Silver
Birches

Also by Adrian Plass

Silver Birches

a novel

INTERNATIONALLY BESTSELLING AUTHOR

ADRIAN PLASS

Previously published as *Ghosts*

ZONDERVAN®

ZONDERVAN.com/
AUTHORTRACKER
follow your favorite authors

ZONDERVAN

Silver Birches
Copyright © 2002, 2003, 2009 by Adrian Plass

Previously published as *Ghosts*

This title is also available as a Zondervan ebook.
Visit www.zondervan.com/ebooks.

This title is also available in a Zondervan audio edition.
Visit www.zondervan.fm.

Requests for information should be addressed to:
Zondervan, *Grand Rapids, Michigan* 49530

ISBN 978-0-310-29203-6

Interior design by Christine Orejuela-Winkelman

Printed in the United States of America

09 10 11 12 13 14 15 • 23 22 21 20 19 18 17 16 15 14 13 12 11 10 9 8 7 6 5 4 3 2 1

This book is dedicated to
Kate, with all my love

I'd like to go by climbing a birch tree,
And climb black branches up a snow-white trunk
Toward heaven, till the tree could bear no more,
But dipped its top and set me down again.
That would be good both going and coming back.
One could do worse than be a swinger of birches.

Robert Frost

Silver Birches

CHAPTER ONE
Loss

There is an old schoolboy joke that goes, "How do you know when an elephant's been in your fridge?" The answer is, "You can tell by the footprints in the butter."

Losing someone you have loved and lived with carries echoes of that silly joke. The one who was half of your existence is gone but, between them – the vastness of her life, and the elephantine, Jurassic creature called Death – leave paradoxically tiny marks or footprints all over your house, your heart, and your life. For a long time these marks of passing are to be found everywhere, every day. Each new discovery is likely to trigger a fresh outburst of grief.

Some of them really are in the fridge. On the bottom shelf stands a carton of skim milk, a small aspect of the scheme that she devised to make sure of losing a few pounds before going on our planned sunshine holiday in late summer. She bought it on the morning of the day before she was taken ill. The carton should have been thrown out a long time ago, but the dustbin outside my back door is somehow not large or appropriate enough to contain the implications of such an action.

Upstairs, on the table next to her side of the bed sprawls an untidy pile of books that she has been devouring, dipping into, hoping to read. One of them was about pregnancy and childbirth. This was to have been the year . . .

Beside the books stands a tumbler, nearly filled with water.

The books should be returned to the bookcase, but the exact order and positioning of them on the bedside table, the sheer disarray of them, is a unique product of her hands, of her attention and her inattention, and will be lost forever as soon as they are moved or removed.

Her lips were still warm when they touched the cold, hard smoothness of that glass as she sipped from it. The amount of water that remains was precisely determined by the extent of her thirst.

She has no choice now but to give up exactness and inexactness.

These tiny museums of personal randomness are all that is left to me.

How many times and in how many ways is it expected that one should have to say good-bye? I assent and assent and assent and assent to the death of the person I love, yet still she phantoms to life and fades once more to her death in the sad ordinariness of an unfinished packet of cereal, a tube of the wrong-colored shoe polish, a spare pair of one-armed reading glasses in a drawer, CDs I never would have learned to enjoy, the Bible that is not mine, its thousand pages thickly cropped with markers that were sown over a decade, but have yielded their harvest in another place, her sewing box filled with "bits and bobs that might be useful one day," familiar doodles on a pad beside the phone, and, buried behind coats hanging in the hall, a wide, dark-blue woolen scarf that, when I bury my face in it, still smells of her.

I disposed of such items as the milk carton eventually. Of course I did. There was never any serious danger that I would descend into some kind of Dickensian preservation mania. The books were returned to their correct position on the shelves. I tipped away the water and washed the invisible prints of Jessica's lips and fingers from the tumbler. It took about half a minute and meant nothing immediately afterward. I noted how the glass shone and sparkled as I replaced it with its fellows on the top shelf of the cupboard above the draining board. It was, after all, only a glass. Tomorrow I would be unable to identify which one of that set of six had contained the last drink that my wife had enjoyed in her own home.

In fact, after the very early and most intensely anguished days I became reasonably good at clearing and sorting and dealing with things of this kind as soon as they appeared, albeit sometimes by gritting my teeth or through little bursts of sobbing, conduits carrying away the overflow of continual grief. The problem was that it never seemed quite to end. Months after Jessica's death I was still having to cope with less frequent but no less unexpected reminders of her life and her death. Some of them came from outside the house, brought by the regular postman, a young man with shiny spiked hair and a brick-red complexion who continued to whistle his way up our front path every morning as if, in some strange way, the world had not stopped turning. He brought letters addressed to Jessica that had important things to say about her mobile phone, or her library books, or which bulbs she might like to order for planting in the autumn, or the amount of credit she had on her British Home Stores card, or the fact that she had come so close to winning eighty thousand pounds in some magazine draw that the act of returning the enclosed slip and ordering a year's subscription to the magazine in question was little more than a tedious formality. I answered the ones I needed to and tossed the rest.

One or two were innocently cheerful communications from friends or acquaintances from the past who knew nothing of what had happened to Jessica. I replied with as much brevity as politeness would allow and tried to spend as little time as possible looking at the letters of condolence that followed.

One summer morning, six months to the day after I had leaned down to kiss my wife's cold lips for the last time, a letter with a Gloucester postmark dropped onto the front mat. It turned out to be from one of Jessica's oldest friends, but it was not for her. It was addressed to me.

Dear David,

I do hope you remember who I am, now that so many people in the church know who you are, and I hope you won't mind plowing through what is probably going to be quite a long letter. My married name (I'm separated from my husband now) is Angela Steadman, but when we knew each other it was Angela Brook. That's what I've gone back to calling myself now that I'm on my own again.

I was in the same youth group as you many years ago when we were all going to St. Mark's, so I'm in my latish-thirties now, as I suppose you must be. I used to go around with your Jessica, who was my closest friend all through school, and a biggish girl with frizzy hair called Laura Pavey. I was sort of blonde with high cheekbones and a goofy smile and enjoyed wearing bright jumpers in the winter and was a bit bossy and talked too much. Is that enough for you to identify me by? It's enough for most people. The bossy bit usually rings a bell!

We only knew each other for a relatively short time after you started going out with Jessica, but we actually did quite a few things together. Decent coffee at Laura's parents' lovely house round the corner in Clifton Road after the group to get rid of the taste of that thin, rank church coffee, quite a lot of Saturday mornings at Wilson's, the café at the top of the steps opposite the station where everyone got together to find out if there were going to be any parties they could crash. Two coffees between five or six of us – if we were lucky! It's just come to me that we all went on a church weekend together once as well, some school or something down in the south I think it was. Coming back now? All very happy memories for me.

Anyway, as you know, apart from Christmas cards Jessica and I pretty well lost touch with each other over the years, but I was very fond of my friend and I never forgot her. I always told myself that one day I'd make the effort to meet up with her again, and with you, of course, so that we could chew over old times. Yes, well, we should just go ahead and do these things and not talk about them, shouldn't we? I know it's nothing compared to how you must be feeling, but I am filled with a terrible, desolate sadness when I think that it's too late now. Having said that, there is one last thing I can do for Jessica, and that's why I'm writing to you.

David, I think you might be very surprised to hear what I'm going to tell you now. You see, Jessica wrote me quite a long letter only a day or two before she died. In it she talked about what had happened to her, how sudden it had been and how serious it was. She obviously knew perfectly well that she had a very short time left to live. People usually do, in my experience. Of course, as soon as I read this I was on the point of jumping into the car and driving for however long it took to get to her bedside, and that's exactly what I would have done except that she specifically asked me not to. She wanted me to wait until a few months had gone by and then write to you. I'm doing what she asked.

Jessica sent me something to give to you, David, and when I managed to talk to her for a very short time on the phone at the hospital she was very insistent that I must take responsibility for deciding how and when that should happen. I was a bit taken aback, as you can imagine. Nothing like this has ever happened to me before or to anyone else I know. But one thing's for sure. I'm not going to let anyone or anything stop me from getting it right – for Jessica's sake.

Before I tell you what I've decided to do I think I'd better just fill you in briefly on what's been happening to me over the years since we last met. We all know what's been going on in your life, of course. I've never actually been to one of your meetings, but I gather they're pretty powerful and helpful and that sort of thing. I, on the other hand, have remained happily obscure – well, obscure, anyway.

As I think you probably know, or knew, but I don't blame you in the slightest for forgetting, I went off and did Art and History at Bristol – absolutely loved it, then I poodled around for a bit before getting a really nice, really badly paid job at a gallery in Cambridge. That's where I first met my husband, Alan. He was up in Cambridge on business one day, and he'd ducked into our gallery to get out of the rain. Blinking rain! Bringing the good news and the bad news all in one package. To cut a long story short, this Alan being a nice-looking, independent-minded, charming sort of chap, we got on very well, exchanged phone numbers, kept in touch after that first encounter, and began meeting on a regular basis. And to cap it all, he was a Christian! Amazing! I couldn't believe my luck. About six months later we got engaged, and the autumn after that we were married in York, which is where my dad had moved to after my mum's death. It all felt so perfect. We prayed together, we laughed together about the same things, we shared dreams about what we might do in the future.

One of our commonest dreams was to find some kind of big old ramshackle property in the country, do it up and somehow make money out of it. A few years later, after both our parents had gone, there was enough money to think seriously about doing it. Well, to cut an even longer story short, after a lot of very enjoyable searching all over the country – marvelous times – we found somewhere. It was an ancient place, and when I say "ancient" I mean it. There were stones in the cellar dating from Roman times, and in just about every century since then someone seemed to have added something to the building. And just to add a little spice to the whole thing, the place had a well-documented reputation for being one of the most haunted houses in England! *And is it haunted?* I hear you ask. I'll tell you more about that when/if I see you.

We bought it. It was a mess, but we bought it. We figured that once it was cleaned up and we'd gone round the sales and bought some authentic stuff to put in the rooms, we'd be able to charge the public to come in and look round the place. It was so exciting and such fun. We had this dynamic girl called Karen who came in every day from the village to help, and within two or three months the thing was up and running. Seeing the very first paying customers walk through the door was an amazing experience. There was still an enormous amount to be done to the house, but we reckoned we could do that as we went along and according to how the money was going. It was marvelous having Karen to help. She was practical, versatile, quick, and all the other things you need someone to be when you've taken on a venture that every now and then seems just too big to handle. And I got on really well with her. We were great buddies, Karen and I, we really were. Like sisters. And all that good stuff lasted right up to the point when she and my husband stood side by side like discontented servants at the kitchen table one cold morning when I was bleary-eyed and barely awake, and announced that they'd fallen in love and were going to go away together. Alan was good enough to explain that he needed someone "more feminine and adaptive," someone who didn't feel the need to dominate him all the time.

I don't want to say any more about that now. It puts my whole being out of joint. I can hardly write the words down without smashing something.

I'm still at the house, and still trying to run it as a business.

Right! That's me in a rather crushed nutshell, and here's my suggestion. I'd like to have a bit of a weekend reunion down here at the house, and I really want you to be part of it. It would probably run from Friday evening to Sunday morning or afternoon. I've still got some addresses and numbers from the old days, but you know how it is. People selfishly get married and move and emigrate and things, without any regard for people who are trying to organize reunions. I'm going to try for seven or eight of the folks you and I might remember best, and we'll see how we go. I gather that these things can turn out pretty dire if they're handled badly, so I want to plan at least a rough agenda that gives the weekend half a chance of being useful in some way, or at the very least enjoyable, for everyone who comes. I hope the idea of the ghosts won't put them off. I suspect the fact that we'll have to share expenses a bit will probably put them off a lot more!

There you are, then. I've enclosed a list of some possible dates. I assume your diary gets filled up pretty quickly – I suppose you're back on the speaking trail by now – so the sooner you reply the sooner I can fix it with the others. If you can't or won't come on any of those dates, and you don't come up with any alternatives either, then I won't do it at all. In which case you won't be getting what I was given to pass on to you. That would not be good, because we are both going to have to face Jessica again some day. She was very sweet, but what a temper! Seriously, this may be the last thing you want to do, but please do it. Ring, write, ask any questions you like, but just do it!

More details when you reply

Love and blessings (if there are some about)

Angela (Brook)

I read Angela's letter once in the clean and tidy kitchen while my single, life-sustaining slice of toast got cold. Then I took it into the dusty but even tidier living room and sat, bathed in early sunlight at the little round table by the window, to read it again.

Since Jessica's death I had barely used most of the rooms in my house. She and I had taken so much time, trouble, and pleasure turning it into a place that suited the kind of people we were and the sort of life we were building together with such enthusiasm. Sleeping, eating, and washing were the only areas in which practical need regularly impinged on my unhappiness. I tended to live in the bedroom, the kitchen, and the bathroom. I only came into the living room to water Jessica's beloved plants. I felt cold and awkward in there. After the day on which I made the horribly sensible decision to clear those little bits of random evidence that proved my wife had existed, I had spent every minute of the next weekend

scrubbing and tidying the whole house with a ferocious thorough-
ness. This wild urgency of intention was probably born out of a need
to remove every distraction from the all-absorbing business of feeling and thinking and grinding through my grief.

The living room got an especially good going-over. It seemed to
me that there was little living left to be done in that room. It was the
place where we had lived and done things – relaxed, eaten, sulked,
made love, argued, prayed, written letters, watched television. Quite
a lot of those things had happened on the long, high-backed, wine-
colored sofa we had so excitedly managed to buy from a shop in
Brighton for a drastically reduced price because it had been used as
a demonstration model. That piece of furniture alone was littered
with memories, some forgotten but no less valuable, like coins lost
in the cracks down behind the cushions. I had been unable to bring
myself to actually sit on our sofa since the day of the funeral.

On that miserable day the sofa and every other chair belonging
or imported to the living room had been filled with people holding
plates of finger food and glasses of wine or fruit juice, the majority
wearing their appropriate behavior as uneasily as they wore their
appropriate clothes. Most were sad but no doubt glad to be reminded
that they themselves and the ones they loved were still alive. I suppose that is partly what funerals are for. One or two of them, those
who had lost partners in the recent past, must have been battling to
survive deafening echoes of their own bereavement. I hated catching glances in my direction from those people. They knew. They
were down there. They were still down there in that dark, cold place
where the wind howls and desolation reigns and no one comes.

"We know just how screamingly, hysterically cosmetic all this
is," their pain-filled eyes said to me, "and we know that the very
ground beneath your feet has been turned into the thinnest possible sheet of ice. One thoughtless, overheavy step in the wrong direction and you will be plunged into such a freezing chaos of despair
that you will come close to forgetting how to draw the warm breath
of life into your lungs."

Much easier for me to handle were those guests who offered more conventional words of condolence. These well-intentioned sentiments really didn't have to mean anything very much. They just had to be made up of the sort of conversational small change that you could comfortably slip into your back pocket with a word or two of thanks.

"Anything you need – you know. Don't hesitate …"

"Must be such a relief to know she was a believer. At least she's all right, even if we're not …"

"We're praying for you …"

Jessica's only surviving relative, short and portly Aunt Vera with flabby arms and a face like an old-fashioned pie, was the best by far. She made piles of sandwiches and cut cake and washed up and made tea and looked consistently grumpy, but she patted my arm very lightly every time she passed and hardly said a word throughout the whole day. I came nearest to crying when I said thanks and good-bye to her that evening.

One end of the window seat beside the table where I sat myself down with Angela's letter had been devoted – still was devoted – to what I had jokingly and affectionately christened "Jessica's rubbish."

My wife had been fascinated by old objects for as long as I had known her. In particular she relished the idea that there were ordinary, practical things that had somehow managed to survive into an age where they were far out of date. Every now and then she trawled charity shops and antique fairs, hoping to discover cheap items to add to her collection. Her personal favorites included a flat rectangular box covered with patterned leather and lined with blue silk, once used by a lady for conveying her prayer book elegantly to and from church, a highly evocative pair of Victorian ice skates, and a small wooden box fitted with an intriguing array of little shutters and screens whose function we had never been able to ascertain. Pride of place was given to a picnic set dating from the 1920s, still in its original box, and in truly excellent condition. Jessica loved to take out the little square china teapot with its matching set of flowered plates, cups, and saucers, the miniature spirit lamp, the lidded tins for cake and sandwiches or chicken, the early Bakelite beakers and the bone-handled knives, still preserved in their set of original paper sleeves, steel blades gleaming as if they had been made and bought yesterday. She had found a road map of Great Britain from the same period, designed specially for that new race of people called "automobilists," and one of those thick school story volumes with a dramatic and highly improbable event involving three schoolboys and an elephant depicted on the front cover. These were propped up against the open lid of the box. Eighty years ago we would have been ready and equipped to strap our picnic to the back of the old jalopy, spread a rug over our knees, and motor off for a leisurely day in the country.

As far as I was aware, Jessica's collection had no great monetary value, although the picnic set had been relatively expensive.

A vivid memory.

Late one afternoon she had arrived home clutching a brown cloth-covered case and looking unusually guilty. She had seen something while passing the second-hand shop up the road, she explained before even taking her coat off, and had made a snap decision to buy it because she'd probably never get the chance to buy one again, certainly not in this condition, and she hoped I wouldn't think she was completely mad for spending eighty pounds on it and she was sure I wouldn't after seeing it because it was so adorable and look, she would just open it and here it was and please don't get mad because she just hadn't been able to help herself and there were lots of little economies we, that is she, could make to pay for it so what did I think?

Leaving aside the more negative and hurtful manifestations of this particular variety of sudden madness, there is something irresistibly piquant about one's partner departing from the habits of a lifetime and then begging to be forgiven for doing it. Jessica was never extravagant with money, least of all on things for herself, even in the pursuit of her "rubbish," and I found it oddly charming that she had been on this occasion. Besides, there was no real option but to agree wholeheartedly with her. The picnic set was exquisite. I had to turn my eyes away from the corner that was still graced by these carefully arranged things. She had loved them so much. Come back to me, Jessica. Only come back, stop this silly dying business, and you can fill the house up with rubbish, spend every penny we have on things that make you happy. I would give it all for one extra week of ordinary days with you, my darling. . . .

Angela's letter.

I read it through again, more carefully this time. Why had I carried these sheets of paper through into the living room? Because it was bringing an unexpected, truly loose end into my life? Something to do with Jessica? Yes. Something about Jessica that was not finished and done with. Something that Jessica wanted me to have. Something I had not yet been given. It was like encountering heat after being frozen, little tendrils of warmth creeping almost painfully through the cold veins of my loss. There was still something to be done. Something to be lived. This was the room where that sort of thing might as well happen, or at least begin.

I couldn't help but smile as I read the early part of the letter for a third time. There was very little chance of Angela being forgotten by anyone who had encountered her at the age of sixteen or seventeen, which was when I had first known her. That "goofy smile" had been capable of reducing every male within the immediate vicinity to a jelly-like mass of simple-minded adoration. The wattage was incredible. A natural honey blonde with electric-blue eyes and a wide, generous mouth, Angela had had the very attractive, slightly bruised look about her heightened cheekbones that some girls are blessed with. In addition, even at the age of sixteen, she had been shaped like a delicious dream – she had certainly appeared in several of mine. She was beautiful, strong, always kind and caring, and she oozed with something that made feeble adolescents like me go weak at the knees. I remembered her being confident and competent, rather than bossy. All in all, though, it had been far too formidable a combination for most lads of a similar age to her, including myself. In any case, much as I appreciated Angela with various significant parts of my youthful being, I was giddily in love with her best friend, Jessica, a darkly pretty jewel of a girl, who captured the attention of my mind as well as my body very soon after our first meeting.

Lifting my eyes from the page, I stared out across my front lawn. In the distance, just visible above the serried ranks of bungalows that marched in three different directions from the bottom of the gentle slope beginning thirty yards from my gate, I could see the tops of the hills that Jessica and I had so loved to walk on. It seemed unlikely that I would ever walk there again. Why would I? How could I enjoy it? I would spend all my time looking for her, just as I had looked for her in the week following her death.

But now this from Angela ...

I needed to be somewhere else to think this through. But where? I made a decision. Folding the letter and replacing it in its envelope I pushed it into my back pocket, went through to the kitchen, flicked the shed key from its hook on the board and left through the back door. Disentangling my bicycle from a miscellany of garden-related rubbish in the shed took a couple of minutes. I hadn't ridden my bike for months. A quick check. Tires fine. Brakes fine.

Seconds later I was pedaling toward the mini-roundabout at the end of our road. I thought I knew exactly the place to go.

The morning after the day Jessica died had been warm and dull, the slate-gray sky heavy with rain. I had left my house and climbed into my car, numb with shock and lack of sleep, to drive unerringly, despite having no conscious plan, toward Grafton House, a large Christian conference center about three miles from my home.

Standing in the middle of countryside at the end of a long, twisting, tree-lined drive, Grafton House was crumbling, ancient, and swathed in ivy. Specializing in such spiritual services as the casting out of demons and the healing of negative memories, the establishment was regarded with deep suspicion by many people living in the surrounding area. Some of them, mostly those who had never actually been there, had built up a picture in their minds of the old mansion as a variation on the theme of Dracula's Castle or possibly Bates' Motel. Unchurched locals with a vague awareness of what I did through my occasional pieces on radio and television would sometimes quiz me over a pint about what exactly went on there. They took it for granted that, being a person who traveled around talking to people about Christian things, I was bound to be familiar with the general philosophy of the center, and that, being a Christian myself, presumably I must sympathize with whatever strange methods they used there. I found those conversations uncomfortable. I certainly believed that demon possession was a reality and needed to be dealt with sensibly and properly, but I also felt sure that single-issue fanaticism was likely to be as harmful in the Christian church as it usually was in any other area of secular or spiritual life. I did know folk who had been greatly helped by visits to Grafton House. I knew of others who had ended up seeing demons under the bed, up the chimney, and coming through the letterbox, everywhere, in fact, when all they had ever really needed was a deeper assurance that God loved them. I usually met these inquiries by mumbling something into my beer about how I was sure they were all well-meaning people and we must be careful not to run something down before we knew enough about it to make reasonable judgments. Then I would change the subject as quickly as possible. Not very impressive. But the fact was that I knew next to nothing about the inner workings of the place. You see, I had never been there for the ministry. I had only been there for the lake.

The lake nestled in a clearing in the woods down behind the center. Long ago, in the days when the big house had been privately owned, the water feature in this secluded spot must have been somebody's pride and joy. Clearly artificial, probably originally constructed in Victorian times, the lake was shaped like a figure eight, with one of the circles half as big again as the other. A ten-foot-wide channel bowed out in a semi-circle on one side, effectively creating an island which, if you were a mere human being, could be reached only by crossing a dilapidated rustic wooden bridge, sadly in need of repair. This roughly half-moon-shaped island was awash with rhododendrons and azaleas, glorious when their pink, white, and purple blooms were in full flower, but abandoned, leggy, and tangled through years of neglect. Willow trees lined the banks of the lake, bowing humbly and with graceful puzzlement to greet their own reflections, and occasionally to salute one of the schools of giant carp that rolled indolently around near the bank on the surface of the water, safe in the knowledge that fishing had not been allowed in these waters for as long as anyone could recall.

Jessica and I loved going there. We were never able to under-stand why this potentially idyllic little corner of the grounds had been allowed to deteriorate into such a wild and weedy state. The lake was far from huge, you could make your way all the way round it in twenty minutes if you were fairly brisk. Yet the only concession that had been made to ease of access was a narrow path that was severely chopped and shaved through the thick undergrowth and long grass around the edge of the water during spring and summer so that a complete circuit was possible. Three flaking, rusty old wrought-iron seats offered a chance to sit and cogitate, one at each end of the figure eight, and one (our favorite) on the edge of the is-land, hidden from the house by a bank of rhododendrons and facing out toward the widest part of the lake. Perhaps demon deliverance didn't pay all that well, or perhaps work on the lake and its environs came very low down on someone's list of expensive priorities, or possibly it was just that the people who ran the center liked their lake the way it was. Whatever the reason, the place was uncared for, to say the least.

On the day after Jessica died I had felt glad that the area around the lake was so untended and rough. It matched the tangle in my soul. I crossed the dangerous little bridge, not caring much whether it collapsed or not, and sat on the old iron seat, trying to make sense of her not existing.

I think it was the stilling of her voice that was the most difficult thing to believe. Difficult to believe, you understand, not just difficult to accept. More difficult even than believing that her body had stopped being a warm, live person and become a cold, inanimate thing. For goodness sake, how could such strength of intention, particularly toward me, be so totally quenched? How could it end so abruptly? How, if she still existed on any level at all, and if she had even the remotest, most obscure means of communicating with me, could my beloved Jessica fail to respond to the sound of my voice when I needed her? Never mind theology. Never mind anything I had ever learned or taught or preached about death. This was surely just common sense. I could not stop being who I was. She could not stop being who she was. We could not be anything other than us. At that moment I lacked all faith in the finality of death, but it was nothing to do with the hope of heaven. It was to do with the habit of living. I leaned forward, elbows on my knees, hands clasped together, and spoke to Jessica in hushed tones through clenched teeth, like a spy passing on messages to someone concealed in the bushes.

"Jess, where are you? Can you hear me? Look, I just want you to be here for a moment – that's all. Please, I can't stand it. Come and see me so I know everything's all right. Please, Jess. Only for a minute or two. Please ..."

Silence. Why did she not answer me?

The lake and all that surrounded it felt old and tired. The surface of the water was still, but something dismally less than serene. It was dumb. Unhelpful. Disappointed. This place was as bereaved as I was. People take time and trouble to build and develop things. They look fresh, cared for, beautiful. The years pass. Nobody cares any more. Paths become overgrown, deep places get silted up and become shallow, wood rots and becomes unsafe when you need to walk or lean on it. People are just the same. Generation after generation after generation of men and women building something good and strong and worthwhile together, only to have it all snatched away when the monster, Death, comes trampling over the garden of their tiny achievements, picking out the plums like a greedy child. Generation after generation. What did any of it mean? A verse of a poem I had read came into my mind.

> I took my daughter to the park last night
> She ran with a shout to the roundabout
> The roundabout went round and round
> But it never stopped anywhere very profound
> It just went round and round and round
> It just went round and round.

Time to remind God of a precedent. Sitting up and resting my arms along the back of the seat, I crossed one leg over the other. This time I raised my voice a little.

"You let C. S. Lewis come and speak to J. B. Phillips after he'd died, didn't you? He just materialized all of a sudden, looking healthier than ever, talking sense. Well, did you do it? I think you did it. You can do it. Father, let me see Jessica. Let me see my Jessica. Please do this for me. I do lots of things for you."

My voice broke slightly as I continued.

"Please do this one little thing for me. She doesn't even have to speak to me. It would be enough just to catch a glimpse of her walking over there behind those trees on the other side of the lake. The quickest glimpse, that's all I want. She could be looking for early flowers to pick for you. She could look up and smile when she saw me and then walk on again and disappear. That would be fine. Father, please let me see her smile one more time. Don't give me a stone when I ask for something good to eat. Just one more time. Please ..."

Tears filled my eyes as I listened to the nonsense coming out of my own mouth. I fancied I could see the words I had spoken skimming across the surface of the lake like flat stones, lacking sufficient momentum to reach the other side, sinking irredeemably before my eyes. I came close to laughing through the tears. What on earth could have possessed me to suggest to God that he should be grateful enough to repay me for all the wonderful services I had rendered to him? Presumably this grief-distorted phase would pass eventually, and then –

Suddenly I was sitting bolt upright, my eyes fixed on a spot opposite my seat, over on the other side of the lake where the path was partially obscured by long grass and straggling undergrowth. There had been a momentary flash of crimson, just the sort of rich, deep shade of red that Jessica had often worn because it suited her dark looks so well. Jessica! Jessica was over there on the other side of the lake! God had answered my prayer. I must go to her!

Springing to my feet I rounded the bushes and took the bridge in two strides, then stood irresolute, my whole body shaking. Would the clockwise or the counterclockwise route be faster? It didn't matter. It really didn't matter. Either way would do.

Turning left I flung myself along that narrow, slippery path with no regard at all for tree roots, overhanging branches, or any other kind of natural ambush. I was mad with desire to prove to the part of my brain that remained stubbornly calm and skeptical that something extraordinary had happened – was going to happen. Jessica was there, waiting for me to join her on the other side of the water. Oh, Jessica! As I rounded the bottom end of the lake the rain began to fall quite heavily. I didn't care. Why should I care? I hardly noticed. On and on round the edge of the lake I flew, elbowing bushes and tall grasses aside, my galloping, frantic speed sustained by the knowledge that very soon that dear, familiar face and figure would come into view and we would talk and hold each other and be together just as we had been for so many years. At last, no more than ten yards in front of me, I saw that flash of crimson clothing once more through gaps in a canopy formed by the branches of an aged weeping willow. The person wearing the garment – Jessica – must be standing inside there sheltering from the rain. She was just there. So close! I covered the remaining distance in no more than a second. Gasping with exertion and sheer excitement, I pushed the heavy, dripping fronds aside with one hand, wiped sweat and rain from my eyes with the other, and stepped into the canopy.

It was not Jessica.

Naturally, it was not Jessica.

It was a small, elfin-faced woman with frightened, bird-like eyes and thinning curls of gray hair. She was about sixty-five years old, dressed in a crimson jumper with two tiny white sheep embossed on the front, an anonymous tweed skirt and sensible brown shoes. There was a sickly pallor to her skin and a dark hollowness about her eyes that, even at a glance, suggested some kind of serious illness. My dramatic entrance into the arboreal refuge she had chosen in order to avoid the worst of the rain hardly seemed to bother her at all. I understood why as we chatted. Some people are so consistently cast in the role of victim that they develop a habit of limp acceptance, a weary resignation to the notion that things will always happen to them or be done to them. Other people will never be significantly affected by anything that they might try to do. Poor little Nora was one of these people.

Her life was like something out of an Agatha Christie novel. Nora had worked as live-in companion to a rich, fierce old woman for the last thirty years of her life. Since her employer's death she had suffered from severe panic attacks, profound loneliness, and a feeling that God was always cross with her. Her doctor, a Christian, had sent her to a married couple he knew who were "experts" in this area. After two or three visits Nora had been told that she was subject to demons of fear, insecurity, and faithlessness. A week of the kind of ministry offered by Grafton House would be just what the doctor ordered. She hadn't wanted to go, but she went.

"It didn't seem very polite to refuse," said Nora, "everyone was being so kind. You don't like to — you know."

I knew what to say to her.

I asked her to tell me about her father and watched the driving rain create a thousand ripples on the surface of the lake as she spoke. She told me how much she had loved and respected him, how gentle and kind he had always been, how very sad he would be if he could see the problems that his little Norrie was going through now. She cried a little. I put my arm round her shoulders. She took an embroidered handkerchief from the sleeve of her red jumper and dried her eyes with it.

"Nora," I said, "I don't know a great deal, but I do know that God is just like your father was, only nicer, if that's possible. When you think about God, give him your father's face. God won't mind. If you ask me, I think you felt all those horrible negative things because your life changed so much and so very quickly. I don't believe there's a single demon in you, and I reckon you ought to think seriously about changing your doctor. Shall I say a prayer for you?"

I said a prayer for Nora. She had another little cry, then she smiled at me, and then she looked at the tiny gold watch on her left wrist.

"Ooh!"

It was time for morning coffee up in the hall of the big house. Mustn't be late for coffee when the people in the kitchen have been kind enough to prepare it for everybody. Just as she was about to duck out into the rain she turned.

"And – and I never asked – so rude of me – why were you here at the lake?"

I stared at her for a moment. Why was I here?

"Oh, er, I came to meet my wife."

"Well, I do hope she turns up."

"Yes."

As I watched Nora scurry away along the path, one hand held over her head in a vain attempt to keep the rain from her hair, I felt as if a part of her pain had been added to mine.

"God," I said quietly, "what's the matter with you? I ask you to give me something and what do you do? You give me a job instead. There are no holidays with you, are there? No compassionate leave.

You knew I'd do it, just like you knew poor old Jonah would swing into action once he got to Nineveh. But, oh, God!" I sighed from the very bottom of my boots. "Why did her jumper have to be that color?" I stayed there for another few minutes, weeping with the rain, puzzled by existence, furious with Jessica and with God for not giving me what I wanted.

I spent some part of every day that week up at the lake. Sometimes I sat and sometimes I walked, sometimes I just leaned miserably against a tree, but always I was aching with the wretched hope that, if I could just persevere with my entreaties for long enough, Jessica might come to me and let me hold her in my arms and kiss her one more time. By the end of the week the madness, if that was what it was, had passed. I no longer went to the lake. I knew – of course, I had always known – that I would not be meeting Jessica there. But as I departed for the last time I felt as if I had left her behind in that melancholy place. For a week or more there was a part of me that missed the madness. It had been layered with hope, however foolish and irrational. Now, even that foolish hope had gone, leaving only the yearning and the anger burning intensely in my heart.

Returning to the grounds of Grafton House six months later with Angela's letter in my hand was a different experience. Weather, for instance. The weather for the whole of that week after Jessica's death had been dull. Morning sunshine is so kind to everything it touches, and, of course, water finds light irresistible. The place was no less neglected, but the lake was putting its very best face forward, beaming happily back at its benefactor. Color was everywhere.

Despite this I found that I didn't like being there. I wished I hadn't come. I had enjoyed being on my bike again. That was bad enough. Then, crossing the rickety bridge to the island, warm and buzzing from my cycle ride, I found myself struggling to identify a familiar little package of nerviness and excitement that was making me feel faintly nauseous. As I sat myself down on the rusty old seat in front of the rhododendrons I suddenly recognized this sensation. Of course, it was how I had felt years ago before going on a date with a girl. One or two before Jessica, and then lots of times with her. Clearly, a part of my brain was recalling the week of hopeless entreaty I had spent here at the lake as a real encounter with my dead wife, and was expecting to meet her now. But it was just a trick of the mind. I wasn't going to meet Jessica. She wasn't here now, any more than she had been then. I gazed sadly across the lake at Nora's weeping willow. It would take a darn sight more than a flicker of crimson to send me racing off round this lake today. I found myself wondering what had happened to that frightened little woman. Had she found a God who smiled at her? I hoped so.

Angela's letter.

I took the newly contoured sheets of paper from my back pocket, smoothed them out, and read the whole thing through yet again. What should I do? What did I want? Did I really want to go to some strange old barn of a place to meet people I probably wouldn't remember anyway, and have to put up with them asking questions and telling me how sorry they were to hear what had happened? No, I didn't. Did I want to risk any kind of close contact at all with the lives of other human beings, the kind of granular contact that might force me to open up again and emerge into the land of the living? No, I didn't. And was that likely to happen?

Glancing up at that moment into the blue and white of the heavens I saw the innocent eyes of God, apparently looking in a different direction. I groaned.

Well, I wouldn't go. I simply wouldn't go. I flicked the envelope angrily against my knee. All right, I would at least look at the idea of going.

Did I want to see Angela again? Well, yes, probably. My memories of her, the tone of this letter, her friendship with Jessica — yes, I thought I would like to see Angela again, preferably not with a posse of other people hanging around. Did I want to find out what Jessica had been up to in those hours before her death? No.

Yes! Yes! Yes! Yes, I wanted to know! Yes! I wanted the thing that Jessica had given to Angela to give to me. It was mine. I wanted it! It was my right! I would ring Angela up and be strong. Simply demand that she hand over whatever it was without any of this silly fuss about a reunion.

I sorted through the sheets of paper and read that final section again. I reflected on my limited knowledge of Angela. I reflected on my very extensive knowledge of Jessica. I shook my head. No, not against the two of them. That wasn't going to work.

Was I practically able to go? Yes, I was. What Angela obviously didn't know was that I had canceled all my speaking engagements for the rest of the year as soon as Jessica died. Invitations for next year were piling up on the desk in my rarely entered study at home. They could pile up all they liked. That life was behind me now. I knew I would have to find some kind of job eventually, but there were no money problems at the moment. Ironically, losing Jessica had seen to that. No, the fact was, I was probably more available than anyone else who was likely to come on a weekend like this. No dependents. Never would have any dependents. No wife. Not ever. Free.

A spasm of raw grief and anger hollowed my stomach and rocked my body. Sod them all! I wasn't going anywhere. Angela could keep whatever the sodding thing was. And they could have their reunion and get drunk and vomit all over each other. Good luck to 'em. I stared across the lake. I had been wrong. One little flash of red would have been enough to send me running again. Oh, Jessica!

Standing and shoving the letter into my pocket, I turned my back on the lake, crossed the bridge, and made my way up the hill to the house. I had left my bike leaning against the wire perimeter fence of a weed-strewn, lumpy old tennis court, another potentially excellent facility that had been sadly neglected.

"I'm beginning to really hate this place," I muttered to myself.

I swung a leg over the crossbar and pushed off with my foot across the car-park. Reaching the drive that connected house and grounds with the main road, I deliberately set off in top gear. Standing on my pedals, I gritted my teeth and pushed with all my strength. Exerting the muscular effort required to gain speed and momentum was an exquisite, unavoidable pleasure. A slight gradient in my favor let me accelerate to something near top speed in less than half a minute. I raced, head down, along the frequently curving drive, oblivious to all but the air rushing past my head and shoulders, and the whizzing hiss of the thin racing tires as they went spinning over the black asphalt.

At the speed I was doing I could easily have hit something on one of those narrow bends. A person walking. A car. Another cyclist. Perhaps, I thought light-headedly, I'll just keep going when I reach the main road. If I were to close my eyes and carry on into the traffic, that would probably be that. Problem solved. Why not? As I approached the entrance gates I was still traveling at maximum speed. Directly in front of me vehicles moved at high speed in both directions. They always did on this section of the road. All I had to do was close my eyes and keep pedaling...

I came to a skidding, dusty, tire-scraping halt, inches from the edge of the road, and had to wait to get my breath and my courage back before setting off for home at a more sedate speed and in a saner frame of mind.

Oh, well, I told myself as I reached the little roundabout at the end of my road, at least I'd made a firm decision this morning. Angela could keep whatever it was she'd got. No reunion for me.

Back home I made a cup of tea, carried it through to the desk in my neglected study, and turned on the adjustable lamp. Taking a pen from the pot on one side of me, and a sheet of paper from the pad on the other, I settled down to write to Angela, thanking her for her letter, and accepting her invitation to attend a reunion of the St. Mark's youth group at Headly Manor on any weekend that suited her.

CHAPTER TWO
Friday

She named a weekend in late autumn, and I went.

Motoring down to the West Country on that particular Friday in November would have been no fun even in happier times. High winds and heavy, blustering rain made driving on the motorways unpleasant and perilous. Opaque clouds of spray thrown up by vehicles traveling in front of my car constantly reduced visibility to a frighteningly low level. Presumably, I was doing the same to the traffic behind me, but I was in no mood for such pointless exercises as balancing out responsibility and blame. Good Lord, it wasn't as if I had any great desire to get to my destination. In my present state I had nothing that would be of benefit to the sort of gathering that Angela seemed to be planning, and scant optimism that the weekend would have anything of value to offer me, except ... what?

As I drove, I glanced quickly down once more at a sheet of paper on the passenger seat beside me. This list of names had arrived in the post a few weeks ago. These were the five people, in addition to myself, that Angela had persuaded to attend her reunion, and I had been prodding my memory about them ever since.

Angela I remembered, of course, and Mike Ford was another name on the list that triggered instant recall. He had been at the same school as me, but in the year above. Mike had been loud and argumentative and quite funny sometimes. A bit of a troublemaker. In my mind's eye I saw a square, large-featured face, with a lot of thick black hair worn very long.

Andrew Glazier. Thin face, serious, sort of tense? Yes, vaguely. These were ghosts of memories.

Peter Grange. I did remember him. He was one of those the leaders got into huddles with. He always seemed very clear about what he believed. Always had an answer to problems. Tall and thin with hollow eyes and a large nose. Yes, I remembered him quite well.

Jenny Thomas. Nothing but the faintest memory of this one. Always doing stuff, helping round the place, but that could have been someone else.

Graham Wilson. Absurdly, the only pictures that went with this name were images of a small, earnest, gerbil-like character leaping up and down at the back of the group in order to see what was happening in the middle. I laughed at myself. It couldn't have been like that, of course, but that was what came back to me across the years.

In her circular letter to all those attending, Angela had put forward some ideas about how the weekend might be organized. As we would be together for less than forty-eight hours, she pointed out, there wouldn't be time for lengthy getting-to-know-you sessions. What was needed was a commitment on the part of all those who were coming to be as open and as vulnerable as it was possible to be, given the unusual circumstances. Various things might help. We would begin, for instance, by briefly filling the others in on what we were doing at the moment. Another idea was that at some point in the course of the weekend we would take turns to describe our greatest present-day fear to the rest of the group. That, suggested Angela, could open up all sorts of areas. Well, yes. On Sunday morning we would hold a brief service of communion, say prayers for each other, and listen to a talk – from me! The most important thing was that we should relax and enjoy ourselves.

Vulnerable? Open? Greatest fear? A talk by me? I sighed. What was I letting myself in for? If only I knew what Jessica had sent Angela to give to me. I had run out of guesses.

I twisted and turned in my seat, trying to get some of the kinks out of my back, and settled down to concentrate on the road ahead.

It was dark by the time I arrived in the middle of the village of Headly. The rain was just beginning to ease. I stopped outside the

Lucky Star Chinese takeout in the High Street to read Angela's directions. I had to admit that, so far, they had been excellent. Last lap.

"At Headly, follow the High Street until it swings left. The Red Lion will be on your right. Take the lane that forks to the right past the pub and climb the hill until you see a sign for Headly Manor at the end of a drive on your left. Follow the drive and park in the yard or under the big trees if no space. Push the back door."

I found the lane and the pub and the sign and the trees. Those trees certainly were big. They included a couple of massive oaks on a slope rising up from the dark mass of the house. They must have been hundreds of years old. As I turned off the drive into the yard at the back of the building I realized that I hadn't even begun to understand how big this house of Angela's was, nor how ancient. Even in the beam from my headlights and the weak illumination offered by two carriage lamps fixed to the wall by the back door, I got a vague impression of one of those houses that grows with the centuries, bulging and widening and shooting out extra wings according to the whims and finances of successive owners. A real pile. Leaving my car next to a broken-up old Peugeot parked at the bottom of the yard, I crossed the cobbles, paused for a second or two to pluck my heart out of my boots, and pushed open the door.

Angela was beautiful, as beautiful as I remembered her. Nowadays the blonde hair was streaked with some darker color, and I assumed she was wearing more makeup than in the old days, but the smile – the smile was the same magical switching on of a bright light that had so captivated us boys as teenagers. When she came to greet me at the backdoor end of the long, narrow kitchen, she was wearing floor-length, twenties-style gray baggy trousers with a square-shouldered short red jacket over a thin gray T-shirt. Her figure was fuller but still exquisite. She looked lovely.

My plan had been to ask about Jessica's mysterious request as soon as we met. Now I knew that I would never mention it until Angela did.

She put her hands on my shoulders and kissed me lightly on the cheek.

"Wonderful to see you again, David. Come and meet the others. They're all here."

And indeed they were. At the other end of the huge kitchen a sitting room area had been created, and it was here that my fellow guests were seated rather stiffly with drinks, waiting, presumably, for someone to kick off the process of becoming vulnerable and open. I swept the nervously welcoming faces with my eyes, searching for clues.

Yes, the serious-looking fellow dressed in a sports jacket, the one with the thinnish face and skinny beard, that must be Andrew.

And there was no mistaking the hooked nose and angular body of Peter Grange. With his hollow eyes and straight-cut fringe of dark, tortoiseshell hair parted in the middle, Peter bore a striking resemblance to pictures and photographs of the tragic Victorian artist, Aubrey Beardsley.

The diminutive, vole-like man in gray, sharply creased trousers must be Graham, but who was the rather anxious-looking woman I had noticed staring fixedly at me when I first came in? She had turned away as soon as she thought I was looking at her. Well, of course, it had to be Jenny Thomas, didn't it? She was the only other woman on the list. She wore a toffee-colored pleated skirt and a cardigan in lighter brown. Her hair was cut in a straight, plain fashion that did nothing to flatter or highlight a striking pair of brown eyes.

Oddly enough, I didn't recognize Mike at first. The hair was just about gone from on top, and all that remained at the back was a little tail of hair, twisted into something like an old-fashioned sailor's pigtail. The square, quizzical face was more satchel-like than I remembered it, a record of repeated excess in those scored lines. Mike seemed quite pleased to see me.

In fact, warm recognition was the order of the day. Most of us acted as if we were close friends who had been prevented from meeting by cruel circumstance. Angela was very good at the relaxing process, but it was an uphill task at that stage. She refilled everyone's glasses, with what looked like water in Peter's case, and suggested that, before going any further, each of us should very briefly say something about ourselves and why we'd come. Perched on the arm of a chair beside Mike, she set the ball rolling herself.

"You all know I'm Angela, and you all know what's been going on in my life because I told you in the letter I sent you. I'm on my own here now, trying to keep the business going with a bit of paid help. As far as I'm concerned this weekend's a little holiday from being alone, and I'm really, really pleased to have you all here."

Graham told us in his quiet voice that he was happily married with two small daughters. His work was something to do with selling animal feed, and he'd come on the weekend because his wife thought he needed to "get away" and he agreed with her.

Mike announced in his very loud voice that he'd been married and divorced twice. His work was doing "this and that," mainly in the car trade. He'd come because he wanted to see everyone again, especially Angela. He joked that he'd also come because he'd heard there might be free booze.

Hilarious.

Andrew's contribution was brief and unsmiling.

"I'm married with one son. I manage a golf hotel near the course at St. Andrews in Scotland, and I'm hoping that this weekend will be useful."

Jenny was single, lived in Northampton, and worked for an international aid agency in Milton Keynes. She was looking forward to catching up with old friends and was feeling a little nervous about our spooky surroundings.

"I sell hats and cases and umbrellas in Harrogate," said Aubrey Beardsley, "and I've come here hoping that God will find an opportunity for me to do something that's very important to me."

It reminded me of contestants introducing themselves on some dreadful television quiz show. In the course of this rather bland list there had been a lot of nervous laughter at anything that might remotely be construed as amusing, a familiar feature of early encounters in most residential weekends. Now it was my turn. Not amusing for them. Excruciating for me.

"I'm David. I was – I was married to Jessica, Jessica Foreman when you knew her. She died at the beginning of this year. I came because – " I looked at Angela. "Well, for the same reason as Andrew, I suppose. I hope it's a good idea. Something like that."

That didn't just cool proceedings for a while. It nearly froze them.

If ever there was a house made for ghosts, it was Headly Manor. Angela invited those of us who were interested to join her for a little tour of her home before we ate, beginning with the vast, low-ceilinged cellar. Here, by the light of two naked bulbs hanging from the ceiling, and a torch brought from the kitchen for the purpose, she showed us the remains of the Roman building that had originally been built on the site. Above that, we learned, a Saxon hall had been erected, only to be replaced with a Norman house by one of William's important lords late in the eleventh century. By the time the seventeenth century was under way, this Norman building had itself been largely demolished and built over, and much of the existing house dated from that period. All around us were clear and visible reminders of all these stages of development.

"It's all a case of money," said Angela, as we mounted the deeply indented stone steps from the cellar. "If I had more cash available I'd make the living areas a lot more livable-in, and I'd get the really old, interesting bits into the sort of state where people can come and see them properly." She shrugged. "But as I haven't got any, it's still all a bit of a mess."

The house may have been a bit of a mess, the woodwork in need of a polish, the floors uneven and creaky, but it was still very impressive. Angela showed us the grand downstairs rooms, the Meeting Hall, the Dining Chamber, and the Library with its secret chapel that had been used during the persecution of the Catholics, and a fascinating carved overmantel that swung open to reveal steps in the chimney leading to the room above. There were ten bedchambers on the next floor, including two dark-paneled bedrooms, one of which contained a four-poster bed and a priest hole – a sort of secret cupboard where fugitive priests once hid – up under the ceiling, its door hanging ominously ajar. This room, the very model of settings for most traditional horror stories that I had ever read, was to be mine for the weekend, Angela lightly announced.

"You'll be all right in here, David, won't you?" she inquired innocently.

"Oh, fine," I replied dryly, "as long as members of your paying public aren't scheduled to come strolling through here early tomorrow morning staring at me just as I'm beginning to surface. They might think I'm part of the entertainment. I think I'd prefer ghosts."

"Oh, there'll be no visitors this weekend," Angela assured me. "This is my holiday as well, remember. Can't speak for the ghosts."

The house was wonderful. As we tramped down the narrow back stairs toward the kitchen I thought how much Jessica would have loved to see and explore this place. Together, we could have made the weekend into a real adventure. Instead, I was going to spend it playing silly games with people I hardly knew.

We came together to eat a very polite meal at the kitchen table. I felt cold and alienated. The spare, conciliatory conversation and the clack and click of cutlery on china came close to driving me mad. I groaned inwardly as the pudding was passed around. Had I really trapped myself into staying here until Sunday? What would this evening and tomorrow and the morning after bring with them? Unless something radical happened this could turn out to be one of the most wretched weekends of my life. Not the most wretched, of course. Oh, Jessica!

I can't help it." Mike's head drooped as he spoke, his body swaying from side to side, like a child dismally aware that nothing good will ever happen in his life again until he's managed to be sick. "I mean, I'm sorry if it spoils your party. We said we'd try to tell the truth, and that's what I'm doing. I can't help feeling the way I do. There's no way you can just switch yourself off, you know."

"And the way you feel is – what, exactly?"

Peter was leaning forward in his armchair, confidently, purposefully, to ask the question. I was curious to see if his way of dealing with people had changed much. Probably not. People don't seem to alter a great deal, even in more than two decades. No, his neat head would still be full of solutions, all meticulously stored and arranged like those tools that hang over drawn shapes of themselves on the walls of garages or workshops belonging to organized people. Divine spanners. Spiritual WD40. Special gadgets for getting at the insides of things so that you can locate the fault and fix it. Leaning back, I noticed that since Peter's last trim, the hairline above his collar was not quite precisely level. One side had had the nerve or the revolutionary zeal to grow a little faster than the other. I felt vaguely pleased, then guilty, then silly.

"It's not anything exactly," retorted Mike irritably without raising his head. "Nothing's exactly anything, is it? Not in my world, anyway. Or perhaps you all live in a different world from the one I have to get up and grapple with every morning?"

"You know, I think I can guess your trouble, Mike," said Angela, cool and composed as she expertly extracted the cork from yet another bottle of the tasty Australian Shiraz Cabernet that most of us had been enjoying. "Your problem, if you don't mind me having a stab at it, is that you've never really recovered from the shock of finding that no one objects to your hair being long any more."

General, genuine laughter. Glancing up, Mike found his attempt at a resentful glare transmuted against his will into a self-conscious grin. There was not an atom of offense in the sweetly confident smile that Angela threw him as she set her opened bottle down on the ancient low oak table in front of the fire. I wondered if he would have taken the jibe from me.

Oh, well, I reflected, here is what one might conceivably call a mellow moment. Perhaps there was an outside chance that it was going to be bearable after all. Wine. Laughter. Fire. Friends. Friends? Mmm. Well, anyway, it certainly was the first even vaguely unifying experience of the weekend.

Our meal had been over for some time. We were back at the sitting room end of the kitchen, the atmosphere considerably more relaxed as people began to realize that the experience of being together couldn't kill them, and might even be fun. Mike had volunteered to be the first to reveal his greatest fear.

As far as one could gather it was something about him being doomed to a life in which he would never enjoy a warm and meaningful encounter with God. The problem was that, before and after dinner, he had drunk rather more than the rest of us. For no discernible reason other than this, he seemed determined to behave toward the rest of the group as though we were all strongly objecting to him talking honestly about how he felt. Angela's flippant interjection had come as quite a relief. There was some truth in what she had said, though.

None of us were likely to have forgotten the famous Battles of Mike's Hair. Sitting here tonight in our new, postmodern millennium that somehow didn't seem to need actual people as much as the previous one, it seemed hardly possible that the length of a teenager's hair could have been such an issue back in the late seventies. Mike had been involved in a number of colorful skirmishes and one memorable public battle with elders and house-group leaders back in those days. They had not considered it appropriate for a young Christian person to wear his hair way down below his shoulders. Try as I might, I could not actually remember the root of their objections. Mike's basic argument had been that God had saved him exactly as he was, and that included all of his hair, from roots to rebelliously distant split ends. Not much of an argument, but all his own, and all he had.

"Where in the Scriptures," I could remember him hotly and

single-digitally inquiring of the mild but lobster-clawed critics who took him on, "does it say anything about men having to have short hair? You show me that and I'll do something about it. What you're really saying," he would add, tearing into those in authority over him with the scything insights of a teenager who is very nearly eighteen months into his Christian life, "is that it makes you uncomfortable to have someone around who doesn't come over as respectable enough to fit your personal pattern of what a Christian should look like. Well, being respectable isn't what following Jesus is about, so, whatever you say, I'm leaving my hair exactly as it is! Why don't you ask the girls to cover their hair? Eh? Eh!"

Gracious apologias of this sort had, inevitably, given the nature of our church, resulted in troubled questions about whether Mike's had been a valid conversion. Phrases like "Spirit of Disobedience" were muttered gravely in connection with him. In fact, an ideal candidate for Grafton House if dear old Nora's doctor had been around at the time.

Watching him wrestle with whatever was attacking him inwardly now, real or otherwise, I was struck for the first time by how strange and ironic and terribly sad it was that no one, all those years ago, had had the plain old-fashioned good sense to see that Mike's long hair was a crucial part of the fragile personality he had just about cobbled together in the course of his sixteen years on earth. His hair was something he had done, a feature that peculiarly and distinctively marked him off as being himself. Besides, I happened to know that he had secretly wanted to be a rock star if "The Christian Thing" didn't work out, or if the two pursuits didn't merge, and growing his hair was all he'd done about it up to that point. What a fuss over nothing. Or rather, what a lack of fuss over the important things. Or —

"In fact, Mike," continued Angela, who, glass in hand, had squeezed her very attractive person unself-consciously into the space between Andrew and Graham on the sofa, "didn't I hear on the grapevine that you were having to travel farther and farther afield nowadays to find a church where at least one person would take exception to your – well, I suppose it's what you'd call a pigtail now, isn't it?"

"I could tell you off a bit if it would help, Mike old man," offered Graham in his hushed, tapioca-soft voice. He raised his hand to his mouth immediately after speaking and coughed a hollow, embarrassed laugh. He seemed faintly shocked at catching himself in the act of contributing to banter.

"All right, all right!" Mike raised a hand in mock surrender. "Very funny. I don't mind you all having a laugh at my expense, but it doesn't change anything, does it? And for everybody's information, I don't go to church any more. Haven't done for years."

There was a short silence. The bark on a lump of wood in the fire crackled, then flared and flamed, sending light and shadow flickering over our faces and bodies.

It suddenly struck me that no one was in charge here. Seven virtual strangers (after twenty years, surely that was what we were) meeting in a house full of ghosts and wine and vague memories with the stated intention of opening up and being vulnerable to each other. Must be joking. Mentally I flicked through the list of drastically altered priorities in my life, the list of things that I was definitely never going to talk about, not even if they tied me down and tortured me. Not that they would, of course, although –

"Let's go back to what you were saying, Mike – about the way you feel."

Peter was leaning even farther forward on the edge of his seat now, sharp elbows on sharp knees, clasped hands with long fingers interlinked penduluming urgently away down near his ankles somewhere. He meant business.

"The – way – I – feel?" repeated Mike slowly, darkly and tipsily, giving every word its full weight and value. "The way I feel, being here with all of you now, is, as exactly as I can bring myself to put it for your benefit, Peter, very, very disappointed."

"Disappointed with whom?"

"With God, of course. Dumbo! Who else? Jerry Springer? Joe Bugner? Oscar Peterson?"

Peter considered this carefully before replying.

"You can't be disappointed with God. God is perfect. It would have to be something about you."

Our do-it-yourself expert had obviously decided to begin, in the grand tradition of do-it-yourself experts, by simply hitting the problem with a hammer and hoping that might do the trick. I could have told him it would not. The vehemence of Mike's reply shot Peter back in his chair as if he had been hit by a bullet.

"Can't? What do you mean – can't? How dare you try to tell me what I can or can't do or be or think or – or anything. Those days are long gone. Look, just because you chose to have taken up residence in that flimsy little three-colored Lego prison we built for ourselves at St. Mark's doesn't mean I have to, does it? Has it still not occurred to you that you slotted it together, so you can take it apart whenever you want?" He came to a stop for a second or two, blinking rapidly. "My God, you certainly haven't changed at all, have you? Still solid as a block of concrete. When I think that I used to use you as a sort of – I dunno – a sort of reassurance."

He sank back into his chair and sipped his wine. I wondered how Peter would cope with this onslaught, but I needn't have been concerned. In the brief silence that followed he was simply replacing his hammer carefully over its shape before lifting down a crowbar.

"Scripture says – "

"Oh, don't give me bloody Scripture – please!" interrupted Mike, slapping the arm of his leather-covered chair with one hand. He sounded as if someone had offered him poison.

I guessed that in Peter's world such verbal structures as "don't give me bloody Scripture" tended not to be part of normal conversational currency. Indeed, the combination of comment and pistol-shot slap had left him pop-eyed and pallid. Looking at his face reminded me of the time when a visiting preacher came to speak at the little service my wife and I used to organize at the local nursing home for mentally impaired geriatrics. We had warned him in advance that the response might be a little less than orthodox, but possibly he had failed to fully absorb this information. In the middle of this worthy person's very worthy talk a fluffy-haired, saintly looking lady who had been sitting decorously by the door raised her head and inquired in a resonant, pleasantly conversational voice:

"Why don't you sit down and shut your gob?"

My wife had giggled more or less discreetly and whispered her opinion that the wider church was in urgent need of this lady's services. She suggested we could earn extra pocket money by hiring her out to congregations who wanted to criticize their minister's preaching but lacked the nerve.

Thinking about my wife was a mistake. It made me want to weep with sick horror at the prospect of going home to face that empty house on Sunday night. Going home? There was no more going home. There was never going to be any more going home. Why on earth had I come when I knew that it would be followed by the hell of going back? I decided to distract myself by rescuing Peter, but before I could open my mouth I was forestalled by Jenny's kindly, lilting tones.

"Mike, you said that Peter used to, erm – well, you said he was a reassurance. That was the word you used, wasn't it? I'd love to know what exactly – sorry – I'd love to know, broadly speaking, what you meant by that?"

"Yes, I was going to ask that," said Graham, twitching with interest like a mouse scenting cheese. "I – I think I can guess what you're going to say, but – well, go on, and I'll tell you if it's the same."

Mike leaned forward to place his empty glass on the table. Nobody moving to fill it up had the quality of a very definite movement. After a sideways look at Angela he picked up the bottle himself and dribbled a small amount of wine into the bottom of his glass. Then he sat back, squirming into a comfortable position and squashing his pigtail against the chair so that the very end of it poked out at the side of his neck. Poor little boy, I thought absently. Poor little Mike. Never got what he wanted from his daddy.

"He was a reassurance because – well, I suppose because he was one of the ones who were so sure about everything." He gestured around our half-circle with his arm. "Oh, come on! We don't need to pretend any more, do we? You all know what it was like. You went along to the meetings on Thursday and Sunday evening after church and you sang choruses and listened to what everyone else said about hearing God speaking to them and what was being revealed through the jolly old Scriptures and all that. And you said a few things yourself in the right sort of language, just to – you know – show that you were a fully fledged member of the club. Did a couple of testimonies now and then – beefed 'em up a bit to keep everyone happy. And you thought, we-e-ell, it doesn't really matter if I haven't felt or experienced all the right things up to now, because other people, and especially people like old Peter here, have got enough confidence and faith and whatever to keep us all going. And one day, I used to tell myself, when the right time comes – 'cause we knew God's timing was perfect in those days, didn't we?" He waited for us to react. "Well, we always said that, didn't we?" Only Graham nodded uneasily. "One day, it's all going to happen for me, and when it does I shall be just like old Peter and everything'll be all right. The trouble was …"

He broke off. I wondered if he was worried that ending his sentence might drive him to a far more significant and final conclusion.

"The day never came?" suggested Graham sadly.

Mike gave no indication that he had registered Graham's comment. He was staring, wide-eyed, into the fire, apparently hypnotized by the blue and yellow flames that skipped and pranced like neon dervishes on Angela's swiftly disappearing birch logs. A sudden violent gust of wind filled the whole house with groans and whistles as it pushed and probed at gaps and structural weaknesses in the ancient building. I shivered, partly from fear of huge slavering monsters coming from the darkness outside the firelight to eat me up, and partly because my back was cold. I had forgotten the effect of sitting in front of an open fire in a large room with no central heating. Mike never took his eyes from the blaze as he began to speak again, his voice much softer and more reflective now.

"Do any of you remember *The Railway Children?*"

"Book or film?" I asked.

"Film," he answered, without looking at me, "the one set at the end of the last century with Bernard Cribbins and that girl who played the sixteen-year-old daughter and then played the mother part when they did it again on television awhile ago."

"Jenny Agutter?" suggested Angela.

"Mm, that's right, that's the one. Did you all see it?"

A low, slightly puzzled murmur of assent from the rest of us.

"Soppy film, really, but it always made me cry."

"Me too," I acknowledged, as an image formed in my mind of the way Jessica would have looked up and grinned at me on hearing what Mike had just said.

"Stupid, eh? Remember the bit when the old bloke – the old gentleman on the train had promised to do something about getting the father out of prison after they'd falsely accused him of something or other?"

"Stealing secret plans, was it?"

Mike looked at Angela.

"Yeah, something like that. It was generally that sort of thing in those days, wasn't it? Sherlock Holmes and all that. People always leaving naval treaties and things lying around. Anyway, in this scene near the end, the mother's got the kids at home one morning doing their lessons as usual, and the oldest of the three – "

"Roberta."

"Roberta, yes – Bobby, they call her. She asks her mum if she can be excused from lessons, doesn't she, and she wanders down through the fields toward the little local railway station in a bit of a daze, as if she's got a vague idea something's going to happen but she's got no idea what it is. And when she gets to the station there's this kind of – atmosphere. Everyone she meets is excited and expectant, but no one quite gets round to actually telling her what's happening. And then this train pulls into the station and there are great clouds of steam so you can't see anything for a bit, and the girl's standing at one end of the platform still wondering what's going on. But then all the clouds of steam part, and there's this man standing there with his bags and stuff. And Bobby – she shouts 'Daddy! My Daddy!' really loud, and runs toward him. And it's ..."

Mike took a deep breath and then sat very still, every muscle in his face clenched against the growing storm inside him.

"And it's what you've always wanted," said Angela gently.

At that, Mike buried his face in his hands and wept. He sobbed and sobbed, that sad little pigtail of his bobbing up and down on the back of his neck in time with the rhythm of his grief.

I did feel compassion for Mike, and I did my best to radiate at least a bit of it. I probably succeeded to an extent. But alcohol-based emotion is notoriously unreliable, and I actually felt rather jealous as well. Fancy being able to let it all out like that. I never could. Never would. Not ever. And look, there was Angela, bright and attractive as a fire herself, kneeling down beside his chair, one elegant, red-clad arm round his shoulders, bringing comfort to an old friend who was suffering.

In that instant I wanted and needed an eye to catch across the room as a drowning man needs oxygen. It was one of the things I had so fiercely missed since Jessica's stupidly early exit from this world had taken them away from me. Those moments when we were able to communicate without words in a room full of other people, hugging to ourselves the knowledge that, later, we would laugh together over the silly ideas that had come into our heads. I knew what she would be thinking on this occasion. She would be wondering if the process we had just been through with Mike would need to be repeated for each one of us before the weekend was over. Rather wearing, if so.

"It certainly won't happen with me," I whispered soundlessly to my dead wife. "I don't want to talk to them about you. I don't ever want to talk to anyone about you. If I do that, Jessica – you might really die ..."

Mike was much calmer now. Jenny had fetched him a glass of water from the other end of the room to sip from, and he was mopping at his eyes with tissues supplied by somebody else.

"Sorry, everybody," he mumbled. "Got a bit – " He waggled his head as if trying to clear it. "I got a bit upset. Sorry. I was just all filled up with wanting it to be like it was – like I thought it was – well, like I always thought it was going to be one day." He sighed mournfully. "Even back in the old days I always felt a bit like those kids in that film. Okay, I'd got a father, but he wasn't here. He was away somewhere. Everyone said he loved me and really cared about me, so why didn't he ever come home? See, in films they can make it happen, but in real life it didn't – doesn't." Some of the strength returned to his voice as he went on. "If God genuinely cared about me he wouldn't be making me wait all my life for the bloody clouds to part so that I can see him and really know he's there."

I think Peter might have been on the verge of saying something in reply to this, but before he could get the words out everything was eclipsed by the most unholy, drawn-out, grinding, agonized screech of a noise, at the conclusion of which the whole world seemed to be shaken to its core by one almighty great slamming crash from somewhere in the yard outside the back door. Peter gripped the sides of his chair, Andrew ejected vertically from his seat like a controlled rocket, and Graham gasped and clapped both hands against his chest as though he feared his heart might try to fly from its cage. I froze.

"What in the name of – ?" Jenny's eyes were like dinner plates.

Only one of us remained totally unmoved. Angela levered herself elegantly to her feet, smiling and shaking her head a little at the expressions on our faces.

"I'm truly sorry if this disappoints any of you," she said, "but that appalling noise wasn't God expressing his wrath, nor was it the devil giving Peter a round of applause. It wasn't even one of our common-or-garden ghosts. I should have warned you. Sometimes when the wind's really bad it gets in through the back of one of the old barns in the yard and pushes the door open so that it screeches across the cobbles. Then it smashes it back against the wall. You'd be amazed at the power of the weather in these parts – that door's quite hefty. I'm sorry, but I'm going to have to do something about it. The stuff in there will get blown to kingdom come."

Leaning across to pick up the flashlight she had used earlier from the sill of the deep-set eighteenth-century window beside her, she tested it against the back door at the far end of the room. Then she turned a speculative eye on us.

"Come on, David!" Taking me by the crook of my arm she hauled me to my feet. "I need at least one good strong man at my side. Get your coat. I'll lend you some wellies. Help yourselves to more wine, everybody. Not Mike. No more wine for Mike. Somebody put some coffee on."

Outside, the weather was throwing itself around like an enormous child having a tantrum. Perhaps, I thought in a rare moment of whimsy, because it wasn't being allowed in. There were only snatches of rain in the air, but the wind was unbelievable. To our left, against the faint lessening of darkness above the horizon, the heads of those huge trees on the slope behind the house thrashed their branches furiously and blindly at the lowering sky. I thought of G. K. Chesterton's childhood belief that it was not the wind that moved the trees, but the tossing of the trees that created the wind. I wanted to share the thought with Jessica, but, being dead, she wasn't there.

Instead, Angela was there, shouting against the racket of the wind, putting her mouth close to my ear, and clearly enunciating every word.

"We have to wait for a gap between the gusts!"

"Okay!"

"You grab the edge of the door near the ground – that's the toughest bit – I'll get the top, then when I give the word, push like hell! Okay?"

"Okay!"

In the first available lull we pushed like hell. The door screeched back into its closed position with less trouble than I'd expected, the big wooden bar on one side eventually falling into its iron slot on the adjoining wall with such weight and finality that it was difficult to see how the wind had ever been able to shift it in the first place.

"Well done, us!" bawled Angela into my ear again. "Now – we need to go in through the side door and somehow fix it from the inside. You hold the flash and I'll have a look round for some rope!"

"No ghosts waiting for us in the barn, then?"

She smiled grimly.

"None that would dare get in my way when there's something to be done, no. Besides, I've had Orkin in. Here, grab this – come on!"

It took several minutes of stumbling and crashing around among boxes and bits of wood amid a sea of straw to find a rope and lash it securely from the inside handle of the door to a convenient iron ring on the back wall.

"There!" Breathing heavily with exertion Angela patted the taut rope with one gloved hand. "If that doesn't hold there's nothing else we can do. The whole blessed lot can come down if it wants to. Let's go and see if they've finished the wine."

As we were removing boots and coats in the porch Angela said, "You didn't mind being press-ganged, did you, David? I didn't exactly ask, did I? Just dragged you off."

"Oh, no, Angela." I injected remoteness into my voice as I stood on one leg, tugging at a Wellington that seemed to have superglued itself to my foot, "I didn't really mind at all – honestly."

She grinned as though I had said something quite different.

"Oh, good. Well, anyway – thanks."

I had no intention of telling her that in those few minutes of physical activity in the middle of a raging storm, I, one of the least-practical people in the world, had felt more real and alive than at any time since Jessica's death. It would have sounded absurd. And it was absurd. Forget it.

M ay I say something?" inquired Andrew politely, his stern, pointed face quite expressionless.

It was a few minutes later. The half-circle around the fire was complete again, the drama of Mike's emotional spilling-over replaced by an atmosphere of drowsy flippancy. A huge plastic container of a popular brand of assorted chocolates, contributed by Jenny, was being passed with pleasurable laziness from person to person. Mike himself appeared to have undergone something of a miraculous change of mood. It was rather disconcerting. After downing the coffee that our hostess had so sternly prescribed, he had managed to get his glass filled with wine again. Now he was joining in with light comments and laughter as though that earlier outburst of his had never happened.

Andrew's question was unexpected, partly because it altered the mood of the evening, but also because Andrew had been even less vocal than me since the group's first encounter. What on earth could he be wanting to say that was so deadly serious?

"Yes, of course, Andrew," said Angela, "go ahead."

Mike managed to waft his glass in Andrew's direction without spilling any. "As long as it's not some juicy little anecdote about me that I thought was buried in the past, mate, because there are one or two hot little tales that are best forgotten." He chortled tipsily. "I bet old Graham was a bit of a dark horse as well. Eh, Gra?"

"Oh, I don't think so, not dark ..."

Graham blushed purple. Possibly he was making an attempt to look like the sort of person who had once been a bit of a dark horse, but it was a failure if so. Not so much a dark horse as a transparent, leaping gerbil, I thought to myself.

"No," said Andrew, still very politely, "I don't particularly want to tell any stories about the past, but I do want to complain about what seems to be happening this evening. In fact, I might as well tell you, my greatest fear is that this weekend will prove to be a complete waste of time."

Crash of gears.

Somehow the politeness made it worse. I sensed the Englishness in our group being turned up several notches. I couldn't tell what was happening to Jenny's Welshness. Into my mind flashed the image of a boy called Brian Robinson who had been in our class at junior school. Brian's specialty was reminding us, just when we were beginning to enjoy ourselves, what a dim view our teacher or parents would take of the mild, junior-style villainy we happened to be engaged in at the time. The problem was that his voluntary policing succeeded in making us – or me anyway – feel both angry and guilty. He spoiled the innocent joy of being bad.

No one in charge. But we all looked at Angela. After all, this whole singular exercise had been her idea, and it was her house. I sighed. Pathetic.

"That's fine, Andrew," she said calmly, "say whatever you want."

"I'd like to start with the things Mike said."

Mike playfully lifted both arms up level with his face like a barrier and ducked his head behind them, pretending to hide.

"Uh-oh! I'm in trouble, folks!"

"Mike, you said Peter hadn't changed at all. In fact, you said something about him still being a block of concrete. I don't want to misquote you. Are those the words you used?"

"Ye-e-es. But I didn't mean anything, did I, Pete?"

Peter waved a hand in dismissal.

"Don't worry, no offense taken. Just glad you were able to – you know ..."

He meant it. Annoying though he certainly had been at times in the past, Peter never had been one to take offense.

"Well," went on Andrew, "I agree with you in a way about Peter being like a block of concrete, or, as I'd prefer to put it, like a rock. Over the last few years he's been like a rock for me in two or three very difficult sets of circumstances. You may not like the way he talks about what he believes, but I happen to know that he works very hard to live it out as well."

It was Peter's turn to blush. I got the distinct impression that he was facing a brand new concept. Could being a good friend turn out to be the most useful tool in his collection? I hoped he wouldn't hang it up on his workshop wall in the gap between the hammer and the crowbar.

"That's the first thing. The second thing is your comment about not having changed at all. Well, I don't know about him, but if he hasn't, then neither have you, Mike. Not one little, tiny scrap as far as I can see."

"Now, just a minute – "

The dispassionate monotone was relentless.

"Earlier on, you said that you were sorry if the things you were going to say spoiled our party." He waited for no more than a beat, then continued, his voice even more ominously calm than before. "Yes. Well. That's exactly the type of deliberately manipulative comment I can remember you indulging in twenty years ago. You trotted out lines like that whenever you found it necessary to trivialize other people and their activities. And you did it so that you could get what you wanted.

"Let's humble everyone else off the stage and into the wings and get them sitting in the stalls so that there's no shred of doubt about who is the rightful center of attention. That's roughly the way it works, isn't it?

"You know perfectly well that there never was the slightest

question of us meeting here simply to have a 'party.' Nor is there an ounce of reality in the scenario you implied by using that term. I mean, of course, in case I haven't made myself clear, the one in which the rest of us are a bunch of squealing, paper-hat wearing lightweights, whilst you alone are gloriously revealed as a person who genuinely feels things. You, only you, are ready and willing to grapple with the deep, dark issues that are tearing your heart to pieces, and, in the process, favor us all by doing the whole performance in Cinemascope. You spent a lot of time feeling sorry for yourself when I first knew you, and you're doing exactly the same thing twenty years later. And that's how you're going to deal with the things I'm saying now, isn't it? In fact, I can see from your face that you're leafing through your little sheaf of options even as I speak. Shall I get angry with him – storm around a bit, or would bursting into tears be more useful? Stick with the sympathy vote? No, I've already used that one up. Perhaps just a quiet, dignified exit with chin bravely held high, followed by a long, enjoyable sulk. That used to be another of your favorite party pieces, I seem to remember. You could come down to breakfast tomorrow morning looking heroic but pale and deeply hurt. Still enjoy your croissants and marmalade, of course."

Our fire had become a bed of glowing embers by now, but the storm obviously had no intention of dying down just because we might have decided that bedtime was getting close. The rain had got going with a vengeance since Angela and I had come back in. It was driving and rattling against the single-thickness glass of the kitchen windows with the insistence of an urgent warning, its weight and rhythm altering as the wind rose and fell, attacked and retreated.

I think we were all rather dumbstruck by the calm, full-frontal attack that we had just witnessed. As for the victim of the assault, I had to admit that it looked as if Andrew had been right in guessing that he would be sorting through all the possible options. I watched fear, anger, scorn, and an attempt at haughty contempt chase each other experimentally across Mike's keen, weak features. Finally he settled for a derisive tone, its mildness, to my ears anyway, wholly spurious.

"If I'd realized that this weekend was designed to be a forum for personal abuse I'm not sure that I would have – "

"You're doing it again."

Andrew still spoke quietly, but there was a stony, white-hot intensity of anger in his voice that was quite disturbing.

"You're doing it again. You seemed to think personal abuse was fine when you were dishing it out to Peter just now. You claimed your right to tell the truth according to our agreement. Well, now I'm claiming mine."

Mike spread his arms wide, enlisting our support.

"I hardly think you can equate what I – "

"You stole attention from people who needed it badly and might not have wasted it as you did." His voice resonated with passion now. "You robbed us! You robbed people less capable of putting themselves forward. You robbed them of time that should have been divided up amongst the other people who were there. We were there, you know, whether you noticed us or not. You moaned then. You moan now. You tried to control God and the clergy and everyone else with your – your juvenile designer moods all those years ago, and, unbelievably, you're still trying to do the same thing two decades later – this very evening. Do you honestly think you're going to sulk or in some other way pressure God into being or doing what you want without any serious effort on your part? No wonder you lurched so quickly from tears to laughter just now. As far as you're concerned, one's just as meaningless as the other.

"Oh, and *The Railway Children*. Yes. Very moving! I wonder how long it took you to put that little speech together. Did you work it out during the drive down, or is it a set piece that you come out with whenever you get worried that no one's taking any notice of you?"

"Andrew..."

Angela frowned as she laid a restraining hand on Andrew's

shoulder. She obviously felt that the situation was getting seriously out of hand. So did I, but I was reluctant to come out from inside, and anyway, there was a part of me that couldn't help being fascinated.

"It's all right, Angela," responded Andrew, "I've only got one more thing to say, and then I'm going to bed. It's this. I said earlier that I wanted to complain about what was happening this evening. Specifically, as I've already said, my complaint is that there's very little hope of us really getting anywhere this weekend. From what I've seen so far all the old patterns and problems that I remember from when we first knew each other haven't altered in the slightest. I worried about coming precisely because I thought people like Mike might still be playing his same old games. I hoped he wouldn't be. Well, he is, and that tells me we're wasting our time."

Abruptly he stood, smoothing his short brown hair with both hands, looking, in that moment, completely drained. His eyes were small intense points.

"So, I shall be leaving in the morning. Goodnight, Angela — everybody. Goodnight, Mike. I'm sorry if I've spoiled your party."

He crossed the room and opened the door leading through to the lower hallway and stairs. Angela swiveled the top half of her body to speak over the back of the sofa that he had just vacated.

"Andrew."

He stopped. "Yes."

"Sorry — just one thing. About telling the truth."

Deep sigh.

"Yes?"

"You came down here hoping to find that Mike had changed. That's what you said. You were hoping he might have stopped playing his games because then we could really get somewhere. You said that as well. Have I understood you?"

Andrew waited, one hand and forearm resting wearily on the door frame to support his weight. He neither nodded nor spoke.

"But you didn't tell the truth either, did you, Andrew?" Angela's voice was certainly not loud, but it was very firm. "You lied about hoping Mike had changed. I'm quite sure you were very much hoping he'd be exactly the same. Parts of that speech of yours were almost as well rehearsed as Mike's. You came here to say all that. You've been waiting for years to watch his face as he listens to that stuff spilling out of your mouth, haven't you? And now you've done it. Does it feel good?"

By not a single word or gesture did Andrew respond to what Angela had said. He stared steadily and blankly at her for what must have been several seconds, then turned and left the room, closing the door with meticulous care behind him as he went.

As for Mike – well, have you ever seen anyone immediately after they've been flayed alive? That was the feeling I had about the poor bloke. By now he was just a crumpled heap in his chair. It was as if those razor-sharp words of Andrew's had sliced away the outer skin of his self-respect. He was raw and defenseless, like a remnant, a piece of emotional meat. Where did we go from here?

"That was so cruel," whispered Jenny after a little while, her eyes bright and brimming with tears, "so cruel and nasty."

Peter sighed deeply. "I'm quite surprised," he said. "I knew Andrew was in some ways a very angry person, but ..." He leaned across to pat Mike on the shoulder. "Mike, I'm so sorry you had to hear all that. It really wasn't fair."

"I ... er, I do think it was more about Andrew than about you," contributed Graham nervously.

We all nodded and made noises of agreement, I think for Graham's sake as well as for Mike's.

"Amazing," said Angela, one hand pressed against her chest, "what can get stored up over the years."

More mechanical nodding as before, except that on hearing Angela's words, Jenny, tissue in hand, turned and looked directly at me, and there was something about the expression on her plain, good-natured face that I did not understand in the slightest.

G oing to bed on that Friday night was a frightening experience for a number of reasons. High on this list of reasons, despite what I had said to Angela in the course of our tour, was the unexpected shock of finding myself abandoned in a centuries-old paneled room containing a priest hole, a four-poster bed, and a very small electric lamp. The prospect of being stared at by Angela's customers suddenly seemed far preferable to an encounter with the range of spooky beings that my imagination began to conjure up as I lay in my large bed waiting for sleep to come. I spent some minutes peering into the dark corners of the room, wondering if I dared get out of bed to close the door of the priest hole.

Those fears passed relatively quickly. What could a ghost actually do?

But I had brought too many things to bed with me for sleep to arrive swiftly. The sour taste of Andrew's attack on Mike lingered in my mouth. It seemed hardly credible that such a heavy cache of bitterness had been hoarded and sustained over so many years. Surely only a temporary loss of sanity could allow anyone to believe that such a viciously concentrated attack was justified after a gap of two decades. The evening had never really recovered after Andrew's exit.

Then there was the whole business of this reunion. All those years ago at St. Mark's there had been a sense of optimism about the future. It was part of being a Christian. If you got married, for instance, you might have problems from time to time, but because God was so closely involved in your life it was bound to be all right in the end. The same applied to all other areas of life. Job, family, faith, health, and anything else you cared to name. Jesus was the divine long-stop, the final defense against disaster, the one who would ensure that we all lived happily ever after. It may have been naïve and was certainly the result of poor teaching, but it was what we had believed.

Now look at us. Angela, a Christian, deserted by her husband, another Christian. Andrew, filled with bile and the need for revenge. I dreaded to think what Mike had got himself involved in over the years. And then there was Peter, still turning up simplistic comments and advice like great clods of earth that nothing fine or delicate had a hope of growing in. Myself, alone, facing a future without shape or meaning. Graham and Jenny – well, they looked very mild and quite nervous but not too bad. Surely, though, we had been hoping that something a little more interesting and dynamic than "not too bad" would have developed as the years went by? All delusion?

I had learned over the years that for genuine followers of Jesus, doubt had little or nothing to do with lack of faith, but on this particular night, crushed by negative thoughts, I entered a very dark place indeed. Trapped between a past that had gone beyond recall and a future presenting nothing more than a featureless vacuum, I stared with terrified eyes at the part of my life that was called "now," and I wondered where God had gone.

Until the moment when I finally slept, I knew that I would never sleep.

CHAPTER THREE
Saturday Morning

What's it like being a traveling Christian speaker, David?"
I shrugged. "Well, first of all, Jenny, I don't think I am one any more, and secondly, it depends which bit of that magnificent title you're talking about. Traveling, being a Christian, and speaking haven't always fitted together all that well. I don't know – it's all so varied. I mean, sitting in hotel bedrooms watching T. J. Hooker dubbed into German is a vastly overrated pastime, but some of the actual contact with people has been wonderful." I braced myself to deliver the obligatory and quite truthful additional comment: "I've been very lucky – very blessed."

It was the next morning. After his extraordinary outburst of the night before, Andrew had packed and gone before anyone else was up. The storm seemed to have gone with him. Last night's raging winds and beating rain had given way to a completely different stage in Mother Nature's wash cycle. The sun was brilliant but purely ornamental in a sky as blue as a hedge sparrow's egg, the air chilled and snappy as wafer-thin ice. The world was clean and ready to be dried.

Morning and breakfast and a change in weather seemed to have cleaned some of last night's darkness out of me as well. I had vivid memories of loving mornings like these and an unexpected, embryonic hope that it might happen again. Jenny was the only one I had been able to persuade into a morning walk. Coated, booted, and scarved until we looked like two Michelin men, we were planning, with the help of instructions supplied by our hostess, to follow the ridge that ran northward for several miles from a starting point at the top of the hill overlooking Angela's house. The idea was for Jenny and me to join up with the other four to have lunch at a "fantastic" pub called the Old Ox, which, we were assured, was to be found nestling in a fold of the hills on the eastern edge of a village called Upper Stark.

"Beware seductive signs to Lower Stark," Angela had warned us darkly. "They deliberately make their pretty little ornamental signposts much more attractive than their dull little village. And anyway, the Ox makes their rotten old pub look like McDonald's. Besides, we wouldn't all be there waiting to make your day complete, so get it right."

Angela, tough as ever.

It had felt strange embarking on this expedition with Jenny. We said all sorts of bright and cheery things to each other as we stepped out energetically up the hill, but there was no escaping the fact that long country walks with women I hardly knew were completely outside any recent experience of mine. My vague discomfort was significantly alleviated by the knowledge that our little capsule of physical closeness involved walking. Like all the best sports and more than a few social activities, walking is essentially a sideways game. Eyes and bodies forward perhaps, but all other important things tentatively sideways – that can work very well. I hoped it would this time.

Up on the ridge the view had been as spectacular as we had both hoped.

"Why is it," I asked Jenny when we stopped to gather breath at last at the top of the hill, "that views across valleys and hills seem to offer the possibility of solving the most crucial and least identifiable problems in life?"

Exertion and cold had brought color to my companion's cheeks and a sparkle of exhilaration to her brown eyes. Gazing out across the valley, hands pushed deep in her pockets, straight hair gathered in by a red woolly hat, she looked much younger and not at all plain. She chuckled.

"Is that some kind of test question?"

"Sorry, it did come out a bit pat, didn't it? No, of course it isn't.

It's just something I always ask myself when I get to places like this."

She glanced up at my face.

"People who ask questions like that usually can't wait to get the other person's boring reply out of the way so that they can answer it themselves. Tell me you haven't got a clever answer all worked out to stun me with when I've finished mumbling something embarrassingly banal."

It was my turn to laugh.

"Certainly not! I haven't the faintest idea what the answer is. Questions are roads. Answers have a habit of blocking them. I think I prefer the questions really."

"I see." She studied my face for an instant longer then turned toward the valley once more.

A panorama of soft velvet shadows and crystalline light stretched away from us for miles before merging with purple hills and sky of a paler blue in the far distance.

"Well," she continued slowly, "my answer to the question you always ask, and do please forgive me if it turns out to be a tedious old block, is that we love views because they teach us a little bit about how God sees things. In particular, that there's much more space to work in than we might have thought when we were – well, when we were down there being part of the view. Does that sound too silly for words?"

"Oh, no," I said. By unspoken mutual consent, we set off along the grassy track that, according to what we had been told, ran the length of this early section of the ridge. "It doesn't sound silly at all." I considered for a moment. "In fact, it might even be rather helpful. Did you realize, by the way, your accent's become more and more pronounced the higher we've climbed?"

"Oh, rubbish! Are you trying to suggest lack of oxygen turns people Welsh? That's an interesting variation on the usual insults. Mind you, if you're right and it has, it's a good job we've reached the top this early. Otherwise I'd have ended up speaking fluent Welsh before long, and you wouldn't have had the first idea what I was talking about, would you?"

It was a few amiable, wordless minutes after this that Jenny had asked her question about being a Christian speaker.

"What sort of lucky?" she persisted, after listening to my elaborately evasive reply.

I pulled one hand from its warm pocket to rub the back of my neck. A sure sign of embarrassment in my case, as Jessica would have unhesitatingly pointed out.

"Oh, well, you know, I get wonderful letters from people who've got something out of what I've said at some meeting. Stories about how their lives have been changed or they've come back to faith or come to faith for the first time. Marvelous stuff – truly marvelous. And I'm all too aware that a lot of Christians would give anything to feel they were doing something so up-front for God. It's been a real privilege, and ... well, that's it really. It's been a huge privilege."

"And what's the downside?"

I studied the grass-covered bumps in the path beneath my feet for a second or two. The downside. What was the downside? You quite often hear Christians talk about the importance of honesty. Very, very important. We should always tell the truth. The devil will be shamed if we stick to the truth. I had said that sort of thing myself many, many times. Unfortunately a commitment to telling the truth is never quite so simple as, say, deciding to always give the correct change or vowing to pay for train journeys even when you know you could get away with not buying a ticket. Some truth – quite a lot of truth – is slippery and elusive like a wet bar of soap. Just as you think you've got a grip on it and you're looking forward to feeling clean, it slides away.

I replaced my hand in my pocket.

"Being me, I suppose."

"I don't think I know what you mean."

"I mean that however marvelous the gospel is – and, despite coming over as such a miserable sod for other reasons this week-

end, I can't get rid of the part of me that still thinks it's marvelous – I never ever was going to match the message." I raised a hand
again to forestall a reaction that probably wasn't going to happen
anyway. "Yes, I know that's the way it's supposed to be. I know we
pay lip service to the idea that we're nothing but useless servants,
and I believe that – in theory. I believe it and I support it as a prin-
ciple. I just – don't like it. I've even repented of not liking it, but it
never quite goes away. I rationalize it all, of course. I'm good at that.
I rationalize everything."

"You do?"

"Well, last year, for instance, not all that long before ... before
Jessica's illness happened, a young couple turned up at our house
one morning, just to ... to see if I really existed in a funny sort of
way, I think. Over a cup of tea they asked me how I coped with being
a 'famous Christian.' They wanted to know if it was hard to avoid
the sin of pride when I heard how people's lives had been changed
or affected by things I'd said somewhere. So I said, 'Right, here's a
question for you. When your postman brings you a nice fat check or
a letter from an old friend, how do you feel?'

" 'Good, of course,' said the female half of the couple. 'Thinking
of ways to spend money's always fun, and we really enjoy getting
news from people we love.'

" 'But,' I said, 'you don't chase down the road after your postman so you can throw your arms round him and thank him for the
money and the letter?'

" 'Not as a rule!' she said.

" 'And why not?'

" 'Well, because his job is just to deliver them.'

" 'But you are a little bit grateful to him – for doing his job, I
mean?'

" 'Of course, yes.'

" 'Well, that's all I ask,' I told her humbly, 'just a little gratitude
for being a postman who does his best to deliver the right messages
from God to the right people. That's all I do, you see.' "

Jenny chuckled into her scarf.

"Goodness, I should think they were very impressed with that, weren't they?"

"Oh, yes, they were ... so was I, actually."

"And God? Do you think he was impressed?"

I sighed.

"Actually, that little chunk of clever-clever dialogue came back a bit later in the year to interrogate me."

"And what did it say?"

"Oh, it said things like, erm – 'I see, so you really are content to be a postman, are you? Genuinely ready to settle for the humble role of one who's vastly inferior to his message, eh? Come on – you're not fooling anyone. It's your talent and hard work that gets the job done. Be honest – that's more like the way you see it, isn't it?' Things like that."

"And your reply was what?"

"I never got a chance to reply. This ... er, this other voice spoke to me."

"What did the other voice say?"

I stopped and looked directly at her.

"Why am I telling you all this, Jenny? All right – it said, 'What did the little boy give Jesus when he needed to feed five thousand people?'

"'His lunch?' I said.

"The voice said, 'And do you think it would have been sensible of him to make sure he had several lorry-loads of bread and fish with him the next time they met, so that he wouldn't have to bother with a miracle?'

"I said, 'Well – no.'

"And the voice said, 'David, all you ever had to offer was the loaves and fishes of yourself. It was almost nothing when you started, and it doesn't work without a miracle, but it's still all I want. Be who you are, love me, and do what I tell you – that's all.'"

We must have walked another hundred yards before Jenny spoke again.

"And that voice – was that God speaking?"

"Yes. Don't know. Hope so. It's a bit difficult to care just for the time being."

By now the path had slanted down into a little wooded area, sodden with last night's rain, where the branches of wind-blasted trees showered us with drops on the couple of occasions when we brushed against them. The wind was less cold on this little shelf in the hillside, but for some reason the last part of my conversation with Jenny had filled me with a sense of chilly desolation. In that state of mind I was pretty well incapable of seeing anything good. The areas of gray rock that broke through the thin, struggling turf on the rising ground to our left looked to me like bones breaking through skin. The trees and bushes seemed bowed and crushed and weary with the endless beating they must endure from every extreme of weather.

What was it one of those clever blokes had said? "To name a thing is to kill it." Telling Jenny about that little inner dialogue of mine had temporarily robbed me of the capacity to believe in it as anything more than the product of my own imagination. I had made it sound too neat. It had become a professional disease with me. Blast! I felt suddenly hot and embarrassed at the appalling presumption of my claim that God might have spoken to me in such a specific way. I wanted to retract it and return safely to the land of the sane unbeliever or the harmlessly nominal church-attender.

"What's that you're humming, David?"

"What! What? Oh, right! For goodness sake, I didn't even realize I was doing it. It was – oh, it's too embarrassing to tell you."

"Oh, excellent! Tell me, then."

By a considerable effort of the will I managed to prevent my hand from straying to the back of my neck.

"Well, if you must know, it was that Queen song – 'I Want to

Break Free.' That's what I was humming. And as soon as we come to a convenient precipice I shall lose no time in throwing myself off."

"Facing up to the fact that you're a Queen fan can't be that depressing, can it – surely?"

"No." I smiled at the thought of resolving the issue of poor musical taste in such a drastic fashion. "I like Queen. It's just that I kid myself I'm in control most of the time, and I didn't even know I was singing. I must have been mulling over the perpetual problem that God and I share. How is this sadly inadequate vehicle – me, I mean – going to be kept serviced and repaired enough to finally make it through the gates of heaven in the end?"

Jenny looked at me wide-eyed. "Oh, David, I'm ashamed of you! I can't believe you don't remember what we used to be taught on Thursday evenings." She adopted vaguely ecclesiastical tones. "We are all, as it were, vehicles, and the Bible is, as it were, a repair manual given to us by, as it were, the chief mechanic."

"Mmm. Don't you sometimes feel there's just not enough vomit in the world?"

The rocks retreated. The trees and bushes perked up a bit.

"Are you going to tell me – any of us – about Jessica?"

Jenny spoke as though she was asking me the price of beans.

At this point the path ascended once more, taking us up onto a rocky promontory from which we could see, way down among the tall trees of the valley, a huddle of houses surrounding a dumpy little church with an incongruously proud spire. At this distance, and lit by the runny-egg-yolk sun that was dripping light so generously over the frozen countryside, it looked impossibly picturesque. How, I asked myself, could such apparent perfection incorporate blocked drains and gossip and animosity and isolation and prejudice and death and all the other things that ultimately make human communities grubby at the edges, however hard we may try to get it right?

"Is that the village we're not allowed to be seduced by, do you think?" inquired Jenny.

Her previous question still floated between us like one of those lighter-than-air balloons. A blue one. She had let go of the string. If I didn't take it, it would float away into the sky and disappear.

"No, it's a couple of miles yet. Look, I'll do a deal with you."

"A deal?"

"Yes, a deal. I'll try to tell you about Jessica if you tell me something I've been wanting to know ever since last night. What do you say?"

Her mouth dropped open. She stared at me with real panic in her eyes.

"Last night? Something to do with me, do you mean? Something I said?"

"No, it was more something you didn't say – sorry, that sounds like one of those awful novels. It was after all that nasty business with Andrew and Mike. Andrew had gone out after Angela said her piece – which, by the way, was perfect, was it not? – and then one or two people made other comments, and Angela said something about how amazing it is that things can last or – no, not last – how they can get stored up for years. And right after that, immediately after she said those words, you turned and looked straight at me. Very directly and specifically. Remember?"

After a moment of paralysis the expression of panic on Jenny's face was replaced with sudden, shocked recollection and then with something much more akin to dull despair. She clicked her tongue against her teeth and groaned.

"Yes, I'm afraid I do remember. Oh dear! What a fool I am. You drive a very hard bargain." Jenny's voice was small, little-girlish, and ever so sad. "Shall we start walking again? I can't possibly answer that question while you're looking at me."

"You don't have to answer it at all if you don't want to," I said miserably. "I'm ever so sorry. Please forgive me. I was just trying to get out of having to talk about Jessica. It's none of my business why you looked at me."

"Nor is what happened with Jessica any of mine. I – I will tell you. Just give me a minute."

As we somewhat uncomfortably continued our trudge along the path I raged inwardly at myself for being stupid. Why did I always find it necessary to complicate things so much? When Jenny asked that question just now I should simply have told her that I wasn't yet ready to talk about Jessica, and that would have been that. She would have quite understood – or at the very least, she would have pretended to understand, and we could have continued our walk along the top of the world in peace. As it was, because of my ridiculous talk of a "deal," we were both doomed to open up on subjects that we would probably much rather keep to ourselves.

What was Jenny winding herself up to tell me? A grimace reached my face as I pondered this question. Please, let it not be another great wound of resentment that was about to open up after all these years, this time bleeding all over me instead of Mike. Good heavens, it wasn't even as if I remembered Jenny that well.

When I concentrated hard, what were my actual memories of her?

Casting my mind back to the days when we all met regularly on at least those two evenings in every week, I made a conscious effort to pin down bits and pieces from a jumble of impressions and recollections. Some were very clear and specific. I could almost hear the rattle of plastic coffee cups and saucers on the Formica-topped serving hatch; the loud echoing scrape of chair legs along the wooden floor of the church annex as pairs of volunteers dragged chairs up from the cupboard at the back and arranged them into a rough semicircle; the slap, flutter and click of Bibles, notebooks, and pens being taken from bags once we'd sat down, and occasional peals of laughter combined with the chattering exchange of recent news as songbooks were given out and we waited for Malcolm, the curate who led our group, to formally begin the meeting.

A spiritual, fairly solemn lady called Ethel, dressed in what always seemed to me depressingly sensible dark green and brown clothes, was usually on hand to assist the curate in a variety of practical ways. Ethel was tirelessly kind, but deflatingly somber about the Christian faith. She dealt with the (to me) totally unfathomable female problems experienced by the girls in the group, and accompanied our singing with strong, well-behaved chords on the upright piano. Ethel and the curate always made a great big thing about never spending time in a room together without anyone else being present, a precaution that invariably provoked a sort of tickling amusement in the less respectful among us. The prospect of our young, skinny, earnest leader and the solemn, pear-shaped, middle-aged Ethel finding themselves succumbing to lurid and inappropriate urges of the flesh in the confines of the church office seemed about as remote as the equally absurd idea put about by some idiot or other that we were all going to die one day.

Other, more complex memories were to do with feelings and had to be teased out of the abstract in order for their real nature to be identified. I realized with a little start, for instance, that the rich, fruit-laden mixture of apprehension and excitement I had felt as we gathered each week to worship a God who might do or say anything right here in that very room, was inextricably bound up with my deep and thrilling passion for Jessica, who, until I started to go out with her, always seemed to be sitting just in front of me, usually between Angela and Laura Pavey, the girl Angela had mentioned in her letter. I had always had a vague feeling in my teenage soul that I would like to tear Angela to pieces with my bare teeth, or something along those predatory lines, although I prayed against such powerful surges of lust with all the fervor of a God-fearing sixteen-year-old. In any case, I knew that if it came to something as distant and unlikely and ungodly as what one might call "the crunch," I would be scared stiff of her. Jessica, on the other hand, violet-eyed, devout, clever, and irresistibly cuddly, I simply adored. I had decided, even at that early stage in our acquaintance, that I wanted to marry her and take up residence way back inside her beautiful eyes for the rest of my life. Later, amazingly, that was exactly what I had managed to do, except that her sudden illness meant it had turned out to be for the rest of her life. Just at the moment there seemed to be an awful lot of mine left.

So, where did Jenny fit in among all these images of the past? It was really not surprising that people like Mike were easy to remember. How could one not remember him, given his tendency to swing from loud, hectoring defense of God to equally wild and blistering attack? Probably, I thought with a smile, God had found it a lot easier to live with Mike's attacks than with his defense. With friends or followers like Mike ...

Yes, there were quite a number of folk whose faces and voices came back to me with surprising vividness as I made the effort to bring them to life in my mind. Unfortunately, Jenny was not one of them. I could call her to mind only as a virtually faceless presence, like someone visible but blurred in the shadowy bit at the side of an old photograph. Or like a person put in to swell the chorus of a production in which, quite naturally at the age of sixteen, I unquestionably believed myself to be the star. Those I cared about and those whose lives unavoidably impinged on mine were the only other ones with named parts. The rest were incorporeal and wispy. I remembered Jenny being shy and saying very little. Beyond that there was only my faint impression that she had been a keen volunteer for all sorts of practical tasks that demanded regular attention, but ...

"In those days I was so in love with you that it used to hurt my tummy sometimes. Well, anyway, I had a terrible crush on you." She set her lips and shook her head angrily. "No! What am I talking about? I was in love with you. I loved you. I dreamed about you and thought about you and dressed for you and foolishly imagined all sorts of things every time your eyes happened to turn in my direction. Why does it always have to be called a crush when people who are plain or ugly or young or simple fall for the good-looking, heavily in demand stars that they're obviously never going to get in a million years? It's not fair, is it?"

"I don't think – "

"Oh, no! Please!" Snatching her chin a few degrees even farther away from me and screwing her face up in anguished frustration, Jenny reached out blindly and rapped my elbow sharply three or four times with the knuckles of her gloved fist. "Please don't say something corny and over-the-top not true about the way I look or – or anything like that. I couldn't stand it! I'm not asking for sympathy or reassurance. I don't need either of those, thank you very much – not about this, anyway. I'm just answering your question. That's our deal, isn't it? And before you ask or don't ask, I'm not in love with you any more."

She hesitated. This time I didn't need telling that I should keep my mouth shut.

"David, I'll be honest – you're going to think me so foolish – I wasn't completely sure that all those feelings had gone before I came down here. I've not had a relationship that's meant a great deal or got anywhere very much since the time when we knew each other … well, since the time when I knew you. Apart from my relationship with Jesus, that is. That's by far the most important one as far as I'm concerned, although I'd still love to get married one day. No, I suppose I just wondered if the warm feeling about you that I've been cuddling inside me all these years was only a memory or … or something else. And, of course …" She smiled shyly. "Of course that's all it's been. Nothing but a memory. I don't want to be any more stupid than I have to be. When Angela said what she said last night I saw clearly how true that was. It's a sweet, silly little memory. And I feel fine about it. Perhaps just a tiny bit bereaved, but – " She clapped her hand to her mouth. "Oh, I am sorry. Do forgive me, that was so insensitive."

Distracted by kind concern, Jenny had turned her face in my direction at last, lips drawn back between her teeth, brows contracted with distress. She needn't have worried. Expelling air noisily from my cheeks, I fluttered both hands in front of my body like a bird flying away – a dismissive gesture.

"No, please, that's nothing. Least of my problems. I'm quite glad really. It gives me a breather to think what on earth I can possibly say about – what you've just told me."

"Do us both a favor and don't bother to say anything. Mind you, if you insist, I think I can supply you with the basis for a pretty orthodox script. I've got quite good at writing other people's scripts over the years. Let me see, now … yes, likely as not, it would go something like this. First of all you tell me how privileged and honored you feel to learn I was so smitten by you. You honestly, honestly do. Then you'll need to throw in a small white lie about remembering me perfectly well, and I guess you'll have to dredge up some small but feasible attribute from the past to flatter me with. Other than adding a clear but subtle indication that you didn't feel the same about me then and you still don't now – just for safety's sake, you understand – I reckon that's about it."

As if by mutual consent we stopped walking, and facing each other for a second or two across the path, we burst into laughter at the same time. Ironically, I found myself struck by the thought of how easily any man might fall in love with the funny, bright-eyed Jenny who stood before me now, but several badly spooked herds of incredibly powerful wild horses fed on extra-strong equine stimulants would have had a job making me say so after that little speech of hers.

"Well, I don't think I'll bother with any of that, then," I said, touching my eyes with the back of my hand as we turned to resume our walk, the atmosphere between us miraculously eased by that shared awareness of absurdity.

"Am I allowed just one other question?"

"Go on," said Jenny.

"One of the things I honestly and truly do remember about you is that you seemed to be forever volunteering to do things around the place. I've got this mental picture of jobs like clearing up and making tea and chairs being shifted and all that sort of thing, and you were always there or thereabouts. Were you just an amazingly helpful type, or am I dreaming the whole thing?"

"No, I wasn't, not particularly. And no, I don't think you were dreaming. It's obvious when you think about it. You see, every time you volunteered to do anything I shot my hand up and volunteered to do it with you. I can see how it must have seemed to you that I was perpetually present. I suppose my silly fantasies included the dawn of romance rising slowly over the kitchen sink. In my dreams you would hold a dripping plate out toward me and I'd take hold of the other side of it, but just as you were going to let it go, you'd look into my face and think how nice it would be to take me out on Friday night. We'd be locked into one point in time, clutching that piece of Pyrex between us as a symbol of our newly discovered passion." She swung her arms briskly and looked out toward the far horizon. "Let's not talk about that silly girl any more. I'm me now."

"And you'd still like to get married some day?"

"Of course. To a converted fireman who's hung on to his body and his uniform. It would be nice to have sex just once before the Second Coming."

I did a little double-take of amusement and wonder. This was nothing like the Jenny that I hadn't been able to remember.

"So, I'd be intrigued to know – what's your response to all those good people who reckon being single's no problem because God's grace should be sufficient for you?"

Jenny snorted and kicked out with her small, booted foot at a stone. It went jumping and jittering along in front of us for a surprising distance before disappearing into the longer grass at the edge of the path.

"I'm afraid I get a bit impatient when people drag individual verses out of the Bible and try to prove something from them. It's like tearing a very small piece of canvas out of a masterpiece and claiming you can use it to tell exactly what the painter was trying to say. I don't think anyone's ever actually quoted that verse from Corinthians to me in connection with singleness, but you're right. You do read and hear that sort of thing sometimes. If they said it to me I suppose I'd do what I usually do when people say silly things."

"Which is?"

"I try to refer them back to Jesus. In this case I'd remind them what happened when Jesus was dying in agony on the cross and he somehow found the mental focus and energy to make sure his mother had someone to look after her when he'd gone. His grace wasn't sufficient for her, was it? Not in the abstract, anyway. She needed someone made of flesh and blood to go and live with. You know, I can't think why we even bother arguing about these things. Is God's grace sufficient to feed the budgie while we're on holiday? That's not what grace is about, is it?" After a minute or so of silence: "What are you smiling at?"

"Oh, I was thinking about your budgie, and then I was chewing over what you said back there about your continually volunteering for jobs at the same time as me being the solution to my question about why you always seemed to be working. You know, I'd never have figured that out in a million years. It reminds me of those games where you're given a scenario that's a bit peculiar and you have to work out how it came about." I considered for a moment or two before making a decision. "Here, I've got one for you. Try this one."

"You haven't forgotten our deal, have you, David?"

Honestly! The whole point of slipping in through a side entrance is to avoid a fuss at the front door.

"No, no, this is part of it. When I was thinking about the old days just now I had a sort of flashback to a time not long after Jessica and I got married. I think we'd probably lost close touch with everyone in the group by then. I was struggling and battling through my first teaching year, Jessica was working hard in her last year at East Anglia, and we were snuggled together like two happy little mice in this tiny terraced house on the outskirts of the magical city of Norwich. Oh, Jenny, we did love that house! The two of us spent most of our spare time cooing over it and petting it and moving things around in it and fiddling around with bits of it. We treated it as if it was a great big brick baby."

I swallowed hard for what must be, I told myself firmly, the first and very last time in this conversation. Fortunately, at this point, the path took an abrupt turn to the right, and our forward progress was punctuated by an unsteady-looking wooden stile set in a low, impenetrable hedge made up of that grizzly, thorny growth that doesn't seem to mind crouching on the tops of remote hills, doomed never to look beautiful. Helping Jenny to climb the stile was an oddly disturbing experience. She took her glove off before climbing over. The act of taking her warm, living, human hand in mine after the things she had just revealed felt, in a confused and confusing way, like a second stage of courtship. Absurd. The second absurd thing to happen this weekend.

On the other side of the stile our way continued in a dead-straight line directly through the center of a vast, bare field that must have held some kind of crop earlier in the year. The width of the path gradually diminished in a starkly geometric manner, until it was no more than a microscopic point on the far edge of the huge, flat expanse. It reminded me of a very simple line drawing my father had done for me when I was little to help me understand the basic principles of perspective. At the age of five or six I was so fascinated that I copied that little sketch out over and over again. And here it was in front of me. Up on top of the world under this enormous sky on an endless path in the middle of a beanstalk giant's field, there was certainly a lot more space to work in than I might have thought.

"I love these massive fields, don't you? Carry on with what you were saying. I like a good puzzle."

"Yes, I like them too. Big fields, I mean. I was just thinking that myself. And puzzles. Right!" I clapped my hands together. "Here's your real-life problem. I'll give you the background first.

"One day Jessica said she was going to invite a college friend to dinner. Someone I hadn't met yet. She was called Claire. Jessica was sure she and I were bound to get on really well because, apart from being very nice, this girl loved getting her teeth into a discussion, just as I've always done, tearing an issue or an argument to pieces, that sort of thing. In fact, Jessica said, Claire was one of the cleverest and most widely read students on the English course at UEA. Apparently she used to come up with these seminar papers that got the tutors nodding enthusiastically and left ordinary, mortal students boggle-eyed and feeling even more ignorant than they'd secretly thought they might be in the first place. Not that Jess would have been bothered by that, I hasten to add. I think, in a funny sort of way, she enjoyed admiring people. She made a lot of nervous souls feel a great deal better about themselves. Sounds silly, but she had a talent for it."

"I remember." Jenny nodded.

"Anyway, Claire duly arrives on the Friday evening or something like that, and, my goodness, what a woman she turned out to be! Tall and willowy and well-shaped without being skinny, long, dark silky hair, perfect complexion, and one of those very symmetrical, strong, intelligent faces. A big presence."

"And what was she wearing?"

"What was she wearing? Goodness! Ooh, dear, let me see. It was a long time ago. As far as I can remember, a dark brownish roll-neck sweater and black shiny leather trousers. I think that was it. I'm pretty sure about the trousers.

"The point was, not only did she look amazing, but every time Jessica or I said anything she listened as though we were propounding some complex theorem that could only be properly understood if you concentrated extremely hard. As you can imagine, it was quite flattering at first to have my inane comments treated with such grave and humble respect, but after a while it became more embarrassing than anything else. She'd sit with her head on one side, frowning and nodding as her huge brain sorted through the small change of my conversation, puzzling over the whereabouts of the gold nugget that surely had to be hidden away in there somewhere.

It did get more than a bit wearing. She was so knowledgeable and so bright. And so infernally modest. It would have been something of a relief to be able to dislike the woman. History, literature, philosophy, current affairs, there didn't seem to be anything she wasn't up to speed on.

"By the time we'd finished our meal around our tiny table in our tiny kitchen my tender young ego was feeling a bit bruised, to say the least. To be honest, quite a bit of the time I simply had not the faintest idea what she was talking about. I just nodded judiciously and produced those little humming tunes that make it sound as if you're mentally sorting through a wide selection of equally valid responses before committing yourself to just one. You can only do that a limited number of times, you know, before coming over as a bit odd.

"So, having eaten, we settle ourselves with coffee in our equally tiny lounge, and it's late autumn, right? We'd had a burst of Indian summer all day while the sun was out, but now it had turned really cold. Really cold. And you know how dank and dismal unheated sitting rooms can be on autumn evenings. Well, we had no central heating in our darling Wendy House, but what we did have was an open fire and a basket full of logs and a bit of kindling that we'd brought back in a wheelbarrow from the wood down at the end of our road the day before. Jessica, perfectly reasonably, suggests that I light a fire to get us all warmed up. And I agreed, but almost immediately afterward – I changed my mind and refused."

"You refused."

"Yes. I used every excuse I could dream up to avoid lighting that fire in front of the magnificent Claire. I maintained that it wasn't actually all that cold and a fire in the grate would get the room so hot we'd wish we hadn't lit it. I claimed to be quite worried about the chimney needing a sweep before another fire could be lit. In the end I brought a piddling little hot-air convector thing down from our tiny bedroom, plugged it in and stuck it on the arm of Claire's chair so it was pointing straight at her. And, of course, Jessica was staring at me all through this with that special blend of irritation and incredulity that married couples do so well when there's company about. You see, she knew I was talking nonsense. She just didn't know why. Why on earth, on a patently chilly evening, was I exhibiting this neurotic desire to either see our guest sit and freeze, or to direct a narrow blast of hot air straight into her face, when, without any trouble at all, I could have laid and lit a nice warm log fire under a perfectly safe chimney?"

"So the puzzle is ...?"

"Well, that's it. Why was it so frenetically important for me to avoid lighting a fire in front of that woman? What was going on?"

"Hmm, it wasn't something as simple as you worrying that you weren't very good at lighting fires, and not wanting her to see you make a mess of it?"

"No, not at all. Though I say it myself, I'm actually a bit of a whiz at the old fire-lighting. It's true that everyone in the universe thinks their particular method is the only sane and effective one, but no, it certainly wasn't that. Look, these are the important clues, right?"

I ticked them off on my fingers.

"Clue one, I was young and not too sure of myself in most areas. Clue two, beyond anything I didn't want to appear an idiot in front of this amazingly sophisticated, intellectual woman who seemed to know everything about everything. Clue three – a crucial one this – I was in my first year of teaching in a difficult school and getting very stressed each day, so I was pretty well incapable of tackling anything that threatened to stretch my mind. And clue four, when Jessica offered to get the fire going instead of me, there was no way I was going to let her do it either. There you are! Over to you. What was my sad little reason for not wanting to light that fire? Buy you lunch at the pub if you guess right."

"You weren't just being mean with your logs?"

"Nope!"

Jenny narrowed her eyes and drew in a deep breath.

"Hmmm … so … there was something you didn't want this Claire to see or find out, because it would have made you feel silly. Correct?"

"Correct."

"And she could only have seen this thing if you'd actually lit the fire. Right so far?"

"Yep!"

She nodded slowly and contemplatively before speaking again.

"Where did you and Jessica keep your old newspapers?"

I looked at her in admiration.

"We kept them in a wooden box with a lid beside the fireplace, and – "

"And I'll bet the amazing Claire's conversation was peppered with references to this and that from the quality press, and in your box by the fire you only had – what? *Daily Mirror,* was it?"

"Worse. *The Sun.* And worse than that. My brain and my confidence had got so addled and sapped by the strain of tackling those kids every day that, believe it or not, I'd even bought the odd comic on the way home. 'Claire, may I draw your attention to a comment by Lord Snooty in this week's Beano that positively cries out for political and philosophical analysis?' Would've been less than impressive, wouldn't it?"

"She'd probably have laughed."

"Oh no, she wouldn't. She'd have assumed that I was doing some very important research into the psychological and social significance of the tabloid press considered as an extension of the child's comic genre. Gosh! I wish I'd thought of that at the time. It'd have been a lot warmer."

"And what did Jessica say afterward?"

"Got cross. Laughed like a drain. Then we went up to bed with our little hot-air thingy and each other. We always laughed in the end, Jess and me did."

Jenny said softly, "And now she's gone."

I swung the top half of my body sharply, involuntarily away

from her. I didn't want to agree with that. I was still with my wife in our little house in Norwich. At the center of this great open space on the top and in the middle of nowhere, walking the path my father had drawn, beside a woman I knew but did not know, how much did it matter what was true and what was tediously, painfully not, who was alive and who was dead, at least until I reached that tiny point at the far end of the universe where my lesson in perspective would end, and there would be nowhere else to go? The truth will set you free, but for what? Seminars on coping with loss?

I cleared my throat. "One funny thing after Jessica died – well, not funny, but you know what I mean. Actually, no – it was funny. It was very funny. I suppose I just thought it ought not to be funny. Sorry, I'm blithering – getting incoherent. What happened was, I was walking along the High Street one day, and just as I was about to turn into my solicitor's office, I ran into a friend – more of an acquaintance, I suppose. I hadn't seen this bloke Chris for ages, and there was no reason to stop for more than half a second just to say – you know – whatever you say in half a second. But just as we'd moved apart he called out, more or less over his shoulder, 'Jessica all right?' And without thinking I called back – 'Yes, she's fine!'

"Hah! So, as soon as I heard those words coming out of my mouth I thought, Oh, no! Do I just let him go, or do I give him the real answer, or what? So I said, 'Actually, hold on a minute, Chris. When I said she was fine, what I should have said was – she's dead.'

"Of course, very understandably, the poor man laughed with the shock, didn't he, as though I'd cracked some hilarious joke. And then his laugh suddenly froze solid on his face and in the space all around his head, like they say hot water freezes before it hits the ground if you throw it up in the air in places like Siberia. He was so embarrassed. Felt sorry for him. My fault, not his. Funny, eh? Black, but funny."

"And – now she's gone."

I resisted a sudden impulse to stop and kneel so that I could lay one hand flat on the earth, something I had found myself doing once or twice recently when I was alone. There was a sense of being safe and anchored when the entire flat of my hand was in such closely aligned contact with the earth, this colossal globe spinning endlessly beneath my unsteady feet in dumb submission to forces beyond imagination. It felt saner to go with it, as opposed to tottering around on top of it. My fear that onlookers would not share this view did, I suppose, show that I was still in the land of the living or, at least, in the land of those wishing to remain alive and at large.

"Yes, now she's gone. Jessica's dead. Apart from the business with Chris that's probably the first time I've said it so bluntly. She's gone. I know this sounds silly, but when you lose someone you get this nagging, misty idea that if you were to just look hard enough in the right sort of places it must be possible to find them. That's how I felt for a while, but in the end I was forced to face the fact that it wouldn't make any difference how hard I searched for her. Even if I devoted the rest of my life to scouring every last tiny corner of every single country in the world I would never find her because she's dead. There is no Jessica to be found any more. I'm not going to see her again because she doesn't exist anywhere."

"Is it too dreadfully crass to make the point that you will be seeing her again in ... you know ... in heaven?"

I might easily have said the same thing if I had been in Jenny's place, and no doubt I would have regretted it as much as she probably did immediately afterward. Her words sent me leaping over some cliff-edge of anger that I'd been flirting foolishly with ever since my wife's death. I pressed a hand against my forehead and clenched my teeth as I spoke.

"I don't want to see her in heaven. I want to see her now! I don't want her to become something that isn't properly human. Something bright and unphysical and non-confrontational and angelic. I don't want to be met by her in thirty or forty years at the gates of heaven smiling ethereally at me and telling me to come farther in and farther up or anything like that. I've never hated all things mystical as much as I hate them now. I want walks in the wood and having to wash your wellies afterward. I want trips to the super-market and arguments over what we're going to do on weekends and underwear hanging in the bathroom and getting into bed to-gether and one of us having to get up again because we've forgotten to lock the back door, and hands and touch and food and clothes and Christmas and talking about people and – and praying together about the future."

A pair of lying magpies flew overhead, pirates looking for plun-der on a freezing, foodless day. I lowered my hand and my head, sighing heavily.

"The dead have to give up their membership cards, don't they, Jenny? They can never belong again. Willing or unwilling, they've gone pioneering off to the next stage, and they're changed by that act of exploration into beings who don't have any place with us and our weather and our pubs and our feeble attempts to say what we feel. How can they do that to us? How can they?" I smiled bleakly as Jenny spontaneously took my arm and laid her face comfortingly against the sleeve of my coat. "Yes, of course you're right. Jessica has gone to be with Jesus, and thank God for that. Just right now, though, I can't rid myself of the notion that they've both done a lot better out of the deal than me. Don't worry." I placed an arm around her shoulders and patted her reassuringly. "It'll all get sorted out, but there's no point kidding myself. I've got a long way to go. By the way, speaking of deals, do either of us owe the other any change?"

Jenny pondered this.

"Are you going to say anything to the others? Only, that was sup-posed to be the point of the weekend, in a way, wasn't it?"

"You think I should?"

"Something, yes."

"And you'll tell them you were madly in love with me over the washing-up, will you?"

"Of course. It'll make them laugh and it might make them feel sorry for me."

"All right then. I will – tonight."

Mention of the rest of the group brought an abrupt end to our short-lived physical closeness. In fact, as we continued on our way, both of us stayed as near to our own side of the track as was possible without letting our feet stray into the straggly, flint-strewn field.

It had been a hard, risky exchange between Jenny and me, but, as my father would undoubtedly have pointed out if I had been a small boy and he had been walking beside me today, despite appearances, the pathway doesn't really get narrower and narrower the farther you go. On reaching the other end of the field, he would have made me stop and turn to look back the way we'd come. I would have been surprised and fascinated to discover that, even after walking the entire length of the path, we still seemed to be standing on the widest part of all.

A ngela was right about the Old Ox, of course. It was perfect. Threading our way in single file down a narrow, tree-lined chalky track that dropped steeply from the main hilltop path, Jenny and I came across the pub quite abruptly. Arriving at any public house for lunch at the end of a lengthy walk on a cold and brittle sunny day is a meeting with an angel in the wilderness, but in terms of location and physical charm alone, this was something special. A pleasingly irregular nest of ancient brick buildings, the Old Ox was set at the base of an angle formed by two planes of the same hill. The original house must have been well over three hundred years old. From our first sighting the place crackled with the warmth that good pubs send out like welcoming rays to weary travelers.

Maybe, I mused irreverently, as I ducked my head to follow Jenny through the low front entrance, the whole heaven operation should be shifted down here. Paradise could consist of an endless succession of relieved, hand-rubbing arrivals at warm pubs on ice-cold days. It could certainly be worse. Temporarily it was hard to imagine anything better, but only, I stipulated sternly to God, if Jessica was allowed to be my eternal walking companion.

Inside, a huge fire blazed in the hearth. The immediate impression was of clean, faded quality. Expensive, threadbare carpets covered the floor. Woodwork and brass gleamed. There was a loud buzz of animated chatter but no shouting, the sort of atmosphere that my father once called "carpeted high spirits." The deeply satisfying *thunk* of brimming pint beer-mugs being deposited on the polished wooden bar was percussion to my ears, and the staff who were pulling and serving the drinks actually looked interested. On a board above the bar a long list of available meals was listed in yellow chalk. The choice looked excellent. Not a fruit machine in sight.

Yes, I thought, not for the first time, if options are offered, I will definitely put in an application for the new earth rather than the new heaven.

Frantic hand-waving from the other side of the crowded bar alerted us to the fact that the other four members of our party were already present. Having arrived in Angela's roomy vehicle, presumably only minutes before us if they had stuck to schedule, they seemed to have been lucky or forceful enough to bag a circular table next to the window in the bar itself rather than in a modern restaurant extension that had been built out into the garden at one side. We made our way over to where they sat in a pool of sunshine. After coats had been disposed of, greetings exchanged, and two more chairs annexed from elsewhere and squashed in to enlarge our circle, I commented to Angela on how fortunate we had been to get such a well-placed table in what was clearly a very popular venue.

She laughed. "Fortunate? Fortunate, my foot! I booked weeks ago. Good heavens, those are the easy things, David."

"And the hard things?"

She thought for a few seconds, staring into the distance.

"Dealing with rats," she said unemotionally, "that can be tricky."

I was quite pleased a few minutes later when Mike and I were delegated to take the food orders up to the bar and sort out drinks at the same time. I wanted to talk to him. I wanted to make him feel better, and I wanted to feel better about myself. A wise man had once told me that wrong motivation is one of the devil's favorite red herrings. Zacchaeus only had to come down and get the tea on. Obedience was what counted, this man had said.

I had been uneasy about my attitude toward both Mike and Peter ever since the weekend had started. I was all too aware that I had indulgently allowed my ever-present misery to sour the way in which I viewed them. A substantial part of me had been ready, uncomfortably like Andrew in his brief, dramatic dealings with Mike, to summarily discount them as meaningless, hollow people, so trapped by the prison of their limited selves that they were hardly worth bothering with. Who on earth did I think I was? And whatever happened to the mind of Christ, a topic on which I had soulfully addressed large groups of people on far too many occasions?

Perhaps all that clear, clean air on top of the hill had brought me to the beginning of a dim understanding that these attitudes were actually indicating an unwelcome return to the way my mind and emotions had worked when I was a much younger man. Jessica had helped me in those days. I had been her ongoing project. She battled and cajoled me into facing the fact that I had developed something approaching a neurotically negative response to what I perceived as self-deception in others. Being anywhere near people who, in my view, were kidding themselves drove me mad. It provoked feelings of anger, affront, and scorn. In the end, I was likely to dismiss them from the highly privileged court of my esteem and tolerance.

It hadn't taken any very profound working out to realize that this deeply destructive tendency was directly related to feelings about my tormented and tormenting mother, who had come close to destroying family life with her insane possessiveness and jealousy toward my father. No wonder he had gone out of his way to teach me about perspective. He must already have been an expert on the subject by the time I was born.

Only those who have personally experienced such horrors can understand the explosive suddenness with which a jealous fit can rip apart a happy hour or a whole day or a week or a month. As a young child it was commonplace for me to witness wild, vicious, terrified invention and accusation from one of my parents, and a response of non-combative, grieving patience from the other. Decades later there were still times when my childhood fear and fury at the foolishness of the adults that I lived with would grip my throat with suffocating intensity. As a human being my mother suffered the fate of becoming a strangely pointless, unreal figure in my memory, amounting to nothing more than the miserably insubstantial sum of her own foolish delusions. If only I hadn't stuck my big foot into the trap of feeling sorry for her as well. Anger and sadness. Siamese twins who can't stand each other. I had asked God many times to take it all away, but he hadn't. Instead he gave me Jessica, and he taught me how to steer round things with sharp edges that would hurt if I crashed into them.

I certainly wasn't about to explain all that to Mike.

"Recovered from last night okay?" I asked as we stood next to each other in adjacent food and drinks queues.

Mike shrugged, screwing his mouth up and bobbing his head from side to side as if to say that, weighing it all up, the whole matter was of little consequence, but his eyes still bore traces of the inward bruising that Andrew's words had inflicted on him. Today he was wearing heavy brown cord trousers and one of those faded black leather jackets that, for some reason, always reminded me of my teaching days. Into my mind popped one of Jessica's interestingly wild generalizations. "Men who wear leather jackets are telling the world that they have no skin." Not a very good idea to pass that one on, I told myself, especially not to someone who had only just lost most of whatever skin he started out with.

"I comfort myself," said Mike, with the air of one who has been up all night composing epigrams, "that when your Jesus delivered his famous Sermon on the Mount, he never said 'Blessed are the horses' behinds.' "

Viewed as the product of a night's work this was a little disappointing on the epigram front, but Mike's comment, crass and crude as it was, struck me as being very interesting. At some later date I would let my mind explore the idea and see where it took me.

"It was an extraordinarily nasty thing to do, Mike. But, look, I just want to tell you that I thought the way you controlled yourself was really impressive. You could have gone mad or – or launched yourself at him or something, but you didn't. You must have been devastated, but you handled it so well. Goodness knows what I'd have done."

He nodded and looked pleased. But why does a revival of good humor so often lead to a blast of unpleasantness from people like Mike?

"Well, of course, at the end of the day, your problem, David, my old mate, is that you can't afford to put a foot wrong, can you? What I mean is, purely on a commercial basis, public sin would be a very bad career move for you, wouldn't it? I guess the invitations would dry up pretty sharpish if you were in the papers for tearing the innards out of someone in public or getting pissed and having to be peeled off the pavement by coppers in Leicester Square. Am I right?"

He leaned across to give me a playful punch on the shoulder. I took a deep breath and managed to make myself smile and nod in response. After all, no one had ever claimed that doing the more useful things would be easy. I had been living with worse things than this.

"I don't suppose you saw Andrew again before he left?" I asked, hoping to change the subject. "He'd gone by the time I got up."

"As a matter of fact I did." Mike rubbed the very top of his head with the knuckles of one hand. "Didn't sleep all that well last night, so I came trekking down at some unearthly hour to make a brew, and there he was, dressed and packed and whatnot, all ready to clear off now he'd done the dirty deed. I thought, well, no point leaving things all up in the air. I know he said that stuff about how I used to sulk, but that's one thing I don't do any more. I don't – honest Injun. And if you say I do I won't speak to you for a week. Joke! So, anyway, I stuck my hand out like a good sport and said some stuff along the lines of, 'No hard feelings, mate. Good luck with whatever you do,' that sort of thing. And do you know what he said to me?"

I was intrigued. "What did he say?"

"He said – I think these were his exact words – he said, in a voice that sounded like it was being squeezed through a chicken's backside, 'Sentimentality is the bank holiday of cynicism.' And then he picked up his bag and cleared off out the door without shaking my hand."

" 'Sentimentality is the bank holiday of cynicism'?"

"That's the feller."

"And how did that make you feel?"

"We-e-ell," Mike shifted his weight from one foot to the other and frowned, "I'm not all that sure. To be honest, on the spur of the moment, what with being a bit worn out and everything, I couldn't work out if it was an insult or a compliment. Know what I mean? So I was left standing there, not sure if I ought to run after him, wring his hand, and thank him, or catch hold of the blighter and smack him one. I mean, I've thought about what he said but I can't seem to make it mean anything. What d'you think?"

"Er, I don't think it's a compliment."

"No, I had a feeling it probably wasn't." He shrugged. "Oh, well, never mind."

"I seem to remember it's something Oscar Wilde wrote in prison. It's from that long letter he wrote to his lover, Alfred Douglas, the one he called Bosie."

Mike whistled in surprise. "Well, swipe me!" he said, "I'd never have figured that Andrew for a woofter."

My head was beginning to spin. Thankfully I was nearly at the front of my queue.

"I don't think he is, Mike. By the way, why did you call Jesus 'my Jesus' just now?"

"Why did I –? Did I?"

"Yes. You said 'when your Jesus delivered the Sermon on the Mount,' didn't you?"

"So?"

"I just wondered if that meant you don't think of yourself as a Christian any more. From what you were saying last night I'd have said it's still very important to you. You were – well, you were deeply passionate about wanting God to be real, about wanting him to be a real father. You told us you wanted all those things we used to say in the past to come true. Didn't you?"

Foolish of me really. Near the front of a queue in a crowded pub was not the ideal place to embark on such discussions. Looking rather embarrassed, Mike pulled a packet from the inside pocket of his jacket. Selecting a cigarette, he tapped it on the back of his hand before lighting it with a bright blue disposable lighter fished out of the opposite pocket. Throwing his head back, he blew a stream of smoke toward the ceiling.

"That Andrew bloke was probably not far off the mark last night, Dave," he said unexpectedly and dismissively, "I was half-cut and just looking for a spot of attention. No real harm in that, is there?"

"Well, no, but –"

"Your turn's coming up, look. I'll get the drinks. See you back at the table. Don't forget my pepper sauce. On the side, not on the steak. Now that is important."

CHAPTER FOUR
Saturday Afternoon

L ater that day I found myself involved in an activity as bizarre and unusual as anything I had ever done. And it nearly resulted in my death.

Never a particularly adventurous sort of person, I was generally incapable of resisting what one might call "leads." Jessica rudely maintained that it was just a case of me not being able to keep my nose out of other people's business, but it was more than that really. In my experience little things could easily lead to great things, and that was precisely what happened on Saturday afternoon.

It seems an inevitable feature of any kind of residential week-end, however congenial the residents, that there is one period – more often than not it tends to be the Saturday afternoon – when a certain bleak aimlessness descends, and the whole affair begins to look like a very bad idea indeed. It felt rather like that after Angela drove us back from the pub. Our meal had been so light and bright with chatter and laughter that it really did feel as though some ill-intentioned magician had cast a negative spell on the atmosphere of Headly Manor during our absence.

No agenda had been set for the second half of the afternoon. Angela disappeared into her office to attend to urgent business matters as soon as we returned, inviting us all to help ourselves from the kitchen to anything we wanted in the way of tea. By the time I came back in from a short stroll around the perimeter of the grounds at about four, it seemed that everyone else must have headed for their rooms to sleep or rest or read. Fires had been laid in readiness for the evening but were not yet lit, and the house was far too big and draughty to offer any real comfort or cosiness in the larger downstairs rooms. I knew, from all too frequent exposure to the joys and sorrows of conferences and church weekends in cold, echoing country houses, that these periods of bleakness were often deceptive. They were no more authentic and reliable as experiences than the sessions of sparkling fellowship and profound identification and togetherness that sometimes followed them. I reluctantly confessed to myself that it was very nearly refreshing to feel such a familiar sense of discomfort, one that was in no way connected with the desolation of loss. I could do something about this problem. The sensible thing for me on these occasions was to have a very deep, very hot bath and then either crouch over any heat source available in my room or simply get into bed for a while and read or doze until something else was due to happen.

Finding the house so chilly and cheerless on returning, my Plan A had been to locate an easily readable book in the library, take it upstairs, run gallons of hot water (please, God, let there be hot water!) into the huge, enameled Victorian bath with the claw legs in the high-ceilinged bathroom just down the corridor from me, read my book in the bath for as long as the heat lasted, leap out, sprint back like a boiled lobster to my bedroom as swiftly as possible before I froze, and then huddle over a two-bar electric fire that I had found in my room, one that may have hummed and stunk like a happy tramp whenever I turned it on, but also gave out heat. Or I might get into bed.

Plan B was not my idea at all.

Intent on completing the first stage of my personal schedule, I pushed open the heavy oak door that gave access to the library from the hall, only to find that not all my fellow guests had retired for the afternoon. Peter was sitting alone at the other side of the room, apparently engrossed in a hardback book that lay open before him on a green leather rectangle set into the writing surface of the roll-top desk beside the window. Curious, I walked over to see what kind of reading matter could be absorbing the attention of a man normally so focused on one very particular aspect of life. I would have bet a sizeable amount of money on Peter's selection having some kind of specific religious interest or bias. In which case I would have lost every penny of my investment.

Suddenly sensing that he was not alone, Peter swung round with an agitated jolt of the head and shoulders as I came up behind him. I felt obscurely flattered on seeing a friendly, slightly embarrassed smile bring some relief to the natural tension in his thin, pale face when he saw me.

"Oh, hello, David, I was just reading the, er, well, I suppose they're the poems I love most. I should say, they're the poems I like more than any others. They mean something to me. I haven't seen them for quite some time. But they are important ... to me, I mean."

"I see."

I drew up one of the high-backed library chairs beside his and sat down. I was intrigued. In my self-absorption I had cast Peter so instantly and solidly in the role of blinkered religious repairman that I would never have guessed at an interest in poetry. What an idiot I was! Just as bad as Mike, I thought. Carefully and deliberately I took a seat in the stalls.

"Who are the poems by?"

"Do you know any of the work of this poet?"

Peter closed the slim volume, keeping his place with one precise finger, so that I could see the name on the front cover.

"Oh, yes, Robert Frost. Of course. American, wasn't he? I think I used to know some of his stuff. There's one about a road in a wood, isn't there?"

Peter's eyebrows lifted in surprise. He opened the book again and handed it to me.

"It's this one," he said, pointing to the left-hand page. "It's called 'The Road Not Taken.' It – it's actually my favorite one. I wonder – do you think you might – could you read it aloud, please?"

"Er, yes, of course."

Sitting very straight in his chair, hands and long, tapering fingers placed in neatly parallel fashion on his knees, Peter gazed out through the window, intently listening as I read his favorite poem out loud to him.

> Two roads diverged in a yellow wood,
> And sorry I could not travel both
> And be one traveler, long I stood
> And looked down one as far as I could
> To where it bent in the undergrowth;
>
> Then took the other, as just as fair,
> And having perhaps the better claim,
> Because it was grassy and wanted wear;
> Though as for that the passing there
> Had worn them really about the same,
>
> And both that morning equally lay
> In leaves no step had trodden back.
> Oh, I kept the first for another day!
> Yet knowing how way leads on to way,
> I doubted if I should ever come back.
>
> I shall be telling this with a sigh
> Somewhere ages and ages hence:
> Two roads diverged in a wood, and I –
> I took the one less traveled by,
> And that has made all the difference.

"And that has made all the difference – all the difference," repeated Peter softly to himself, still staring out of the window and remaining motionless, as though he was hearing the whole of the poem over again in his head.

After that a lengthy silence fell. Not an empty one. It was one of those silences that David Attenborough would have understood. It was the kind of concentrated stillness that you have to maintain if you are hoping to see rare, timid creatures emerge from cover when they finally feel unthreatened and safe.

"Why is that particular poem so special to you?" I asked eventually.

Peter's whole being seemed to tighten and coil itself. I sensed that a crucial decision of some sort was being made. The nervously balanced head jerked round in my direction, the sensitive lips twitching a rehearsal of the words he was about to speak.

"Do you have a favorite tree?" he inquired.

I did my best to sound as though personal tree preference was a perfectly logical and reasonable direction for our conversation to take.

"Well, yes, I suppose I like oaks and beech trees, and I've always rather fancied hornbeams because they've got funny leaves. What about you?"

"Silver birch," he replied, his eyes beneath their heavy lids seeming to burn with the fear of self-revelation. "There's one other poem – a longer one."

Reaching across with sudden eagerness, he took the book from my hands. After flicking through the pages for a moment, he handed it back and, without another word, resumed his listening position. Fair enough, I thought, here we go again. Oh, well, I had always enjoyed reading poetry aloud. This one was simply called "Birches."

> When I see birches bend to left and right
> Across the lines of straighter darker trees,
> I like to think some boy's been swinging them.
> But swinging doesn't bend them down to stay
> As ice storms do. Often you must have seen them
> Loaded with ice a sunny winter morning
> After a rain. They click upon themselves
> As the breeze rises, and turn many-colored
> As the stir cracks and crazes their enamel.
> Soon the sun's warmth makes them shed crystal shells
> Shattering and avalanching on the snow crust –
> Such heaps of broken glass to sweep away
> You'd think the inner dome of heaven had fallen.

They are dragged to the withered bracken by the load,
And they seem not to break; though once they are bowed
So low for long, they never right themselves:
You may see their trunks arching in the woods
Years afterwards, trailing their leaves on the ground,
Like girls on hands and knees that throw their hair
Before them over their heads to dry in the sun.
But I was going to say when Truth broke in
With all her matter of fact about the ice storm,
I should prefer to have some boy bend them
As he went out and in to fetch the cows –
Some boy too far from town to learn baseball,
Whose only play was what he found himself,
Summer or winter, and could play alone.
One by one he subdued his father's trees
By riding them down over and over again
Until he took the stiffness out of them,
And not one but hung limp, not one was left
For him to conquer. He learned all there was
To learn about not launching out too soon
And so not carrying the tree away
Clear to the ground. He always kept his poise
To the top branches, climbing carefully
With the same pains you use to fill a cup
Up to the brim, and even above the brim.
Then he flung outward, feet first, with a swish,
Kicking his way down through the air to the ground.
So was I once myself a swinger of birches.
And so I dream of going back to be.
It's when I'm weary of considerations,
And life is too much like a pathless wood
Where your face burns and tickles with the cobwebs
Broken across it, and one eye is weeping
From a twig's having lashed across it open.

I'd like to get away from earth awhile
And then come back to it and begin over.
May no fate willfully misunderstand me
And half grant what I wish and snatch me away
Not to return. Earth's the right place for love:
I don't know where it's likely to go better.
I'd like to go by climbing a birch tree,
And climb black branches up a snow-white trunk
Toward heaven, till the tree could bear no more,
But dipped its top and set me down again.
That would be good both going and coming back.
One could do worse than be a swinger of birches.

I closed the book and laid it gently down on the desk. Was that it, then? Should I tiptoe out of the cold library now toward my hot bath and leave this man alone to deal with whatever intense emotion had him in its grip? Or was there something else for me to do? He turned toward me once more, the expression of terrified entreaty on his face so plaintively vulnerable that I think I would have agreed to almost anything if it had been guaranteed to bring peace to his soul.

"David, I've always wanted to do it. I've never done it. Will you ... will you do it with me now? This afternoon?"

My wife had always maintained that if you were going to be sacrificial you needed to do it extravagantly. Mentally I slammed shut the readable book I might have found in the library, turned off the tap from which lashings of steaming hot water were gushing into the bath, pulled the plug of the electric fire from its socket, and bowed, not to the inevitable, but to the divinely optional.

"Okay, Peter," I said, springing to my feet with all the enthusiasm that I could muster, "go and put three jumpers and a pair of jeans on, I'll do the same, see you in the hall in five minutes, and then we'll go and do it. Right now!"

Peter had not brought a pair of jeans to Headly Manor with him. My suspicion was that he did not own a pair of jeans. He probably never had owned a pair of jeans. Even as a teenager he had usually turned up for church or the youth group wearing a tie with sports jacket and trousers, or even a suit. When he reappeared in the hall, claiming to be ready for our expedition, he was wearing what must have been his third-newest pair of gray trousers, a thick black jumper over a thin black jumper over a navy-blue roll-neck T-shirt, and – a smart jacket. I sternly commanded him to return to his room and place his jacket back on its hanger. Two minutes later, armed with the large torch from my car in case we were still out when it got really dark, we set off.

During my walk around the grounds earlier that afternoon I had noticed a line of birches. They tripped like skinny schoolgirls along the edge of a wood that formed one of the boundaries of Angela's property, running more or less at right angles to the road. I had never considered the idea of swinging from birches, but I had been noticing them all my life. As a small child I knew that they were made of solid silver. I dreamed of cutting one with a saw and running my fingers over the cold, shining metal surfaces that would be revealed. There were three silver birches in our garden. We were rich. If all else failed we could chop them up and sell the pieces for a fortune. Silver logs. As an adult I still believed that they were made of silver. The things you knew as a child may turn out to be factually incorrect, but that is a mere detail. They are true forever.

Something, possibly involvement in such an apparently secular activity, seemed to have atrophied Peter's powers of conversation as we tramped through long, wet grass toward the darkening wood. There was no doubting his excitement though. At the sight of those trees looming like a row of spidery ghosts in the gathering dusk, he turned to me and simply said, "Aah!"

This was something he really did want to do. But why? I assumed that I would soon find out.

"Right!" I said, as we finally arrived at our destination. I slapped the nearest trunk with one hand and gestured toward the next in line with the other. "These two do?"

"Yes, they'll do very well indeed, thank you." Peter nodded like a toy dog in the back of a car. Moving to the tree I had indicated, he stood at the base of the trunk, gazing wonderingly upward like Jack about to climb his beanstalk. I shone my torch so that he could see clearly where to put his hands and feet for the first part of the ascent. It struck me that there was something ineffably Victorian about Peter's long-legged, angular silhouette. As he began to haul himself up, even in his "suitable" clothes, he still managed to look like a man in a frock-coat climbing a steeple.

I watched for a moment and then nervously began my own climb.

I discovered that silver birch trees are easier to climb than one might have supposed. The whippy black branches that occur at closely spaced intervals along their paper-white length are flexible but don't snap. At the point where they actually join the trunk they are surprisingly strong and unbending beneath the weight of an average-sized person like me. Despite my strenuously role-played enthusiasm in response to Peter's request, I had approached this extraordinary adventure with quite a lot of trepidation. Poems are recollections in moments of tranquility. Real life can turn out to be wet and sharp and scary. It can mess your hair up and make you breathe heavily and graze your knees. Finding that these particular trees were so simple and safe to climb was a great relief – for a while.

We reached the top of our respective trees at about the same time. It seemed terribly high to me. This was crazy! After getting my breath back I called out to Peter:

"Shall we let go at the same time?"

"Right! Ready – steady – go!"

Taking a deep breath I released my feet and kicked out into nothingness. The top of the tree descended for a matter of five or six feet then stopped. It seemed that I was suspended in mid-air until either my arms gave way or the tree snapped or the fire brigade arrived. Gasping for breath, bouncing gently and hanging on to the slender top end of the trunk for dear life with both hands, I bent my chin to my chest and peered down between my dangling feet. That carpet of leaf-mould and bits of dead wood down there must be the ground, and it was more than twenty feet away. I bit my lip and swore. Finding that that didn't do me any good, I prayed.

Peter had let go with his feet a fraction of a second after me. The main difference was that his tree behaved itself. His tree must have read the poem. From my position of increasingly serious danger high above the ground, I was just about aware that my fellow swinger had made the perfect, graceful descent, landing lightly on his feet and then releasing the top of his silver birch so that it sprang gratefully back into its natural growing posture. He was standing down there below me now. Even in the fast-fading light I could see that his normally pale face was flushed with triumph and exhilaration as he gazed upward, waiting for me to join him.

"I'm stuck!" I bawled. "The bloody thing refuses to bend any more!"

"I'm gay!" he yelled back, as though my hoarse, panic-stricken cry was merely an attempt to initiate an exchange of personal information.

If I had given in to the urge to burst into hysterical laughter at this point I am convinced that I would have lost my grip and been killed or badly injured by the fall. Even at this moment of imminent disaster a picture flashed into my mind of Jessica, helpless and weeping with laughter as I described the context within which my latest counseling session had been conducted. What comforting words should I scream at Peter immediately before plummeting to my death at his feet? I saw him freeze suddenly, cupping his face in those long tapering hands, wide-eyed with fear as the realization of what might be about to happen to me struck him for the first time. Ducking down, he located the torch that I had left in the grass near the base of my tree, switched it on, and carefully directed the powerful beam straight upward into my eyes.

"Does that help?" he shouted.

"No!" I screamed. "It bloody well – "

If the tree that my bruised and whitened knuckles were clenched around had not chosen that moment to stop kidding and lower me slowly down to the ground, I would undoubtedly have died in mid-chortle that chilly afternoon. The thought of Peter shining my torch so that I would have the inestimable benefit of being able to actually witness the moment when my hands parted company with my uncooperative tree was as funny two seconds before dying as it would have been at any other time. As it was I ended up prostrate on the damp grass, unharmed but limply incapable of controlling successive gusts of hysterical, relieved laughter. Peter joined in, thank goodness, though I don't think he had much idea of what we were laughing about.

A few minutes later, as we trudged back through the darkness toward the lights of the big house, I said, "So you're gay, Peter."

"Yes," he replied with brittle calm. "Pretty well ever since I can remember I've known that I was a homosexual. When I was a teenager I became a Christian and read the Bible. It seemed to say that God doesn't want people to – you know – actually live out a homosexual lifestyle, so I asked him again and again and again to make me not be one. Over and over again. All night sometimes. Crying and asking. That prayer was never – has never been answered. I don't mind. I mean, I do mind very much, but I don't mind God doing whatever he wants to do – or not do. He's God and I'm only me. So I had to make a choice."

"Two roads."

"Yes. We did the poem at school one day. I took the book home and read the poem to myself many, many times until I nearly knew it by heart. I knew I had to choose, so I did. I chose to go on being me but not do anything about it – if you know what I mean."

"It must have been so hard."

He cleared his throat.

"Two main hard things. One is when people at church talk about being gay. They talk about the problem – the issue of homosexuality.

The things they say are hard and – and not really understanding. Jokes sometimes. You sit there and you nod and say yes or no and laugh or frown whenever they do, and wish you could be somewhere else. You feel like a dirty thing. And you're not. You're not an issue or a problem. You're you. You just want to – to be loved."

"And the other hard thing?"

We walked several more steps before Peter spoke again. The swish-swish of our passage through the lush, damp grass was like the amplified beating of a heart.

"Never to, er, love someone – you know – love someone. Never once. Thinking of that has been very hard. But Jesus gave up everything as well. The way for me to get through has been to ... well, to look at him all the time. Yes, all the time. I know it makes me a bit ... but I don't mind."

"And the birch swinging?"

I switched the torch on just so that I could see his smile. It was worth it.

"David, it was wonderful. Ever since I first read that poem when I was sixteen I've wanted to do it. To leave the earth and go up and up and up toward heaven and then be allowed to come back again by flying through the air. And now I've done it. Thank you! Thank you! You see, I came to this weekend having made up my mind that I was going to tell someone at last – about me, I mean. And then, earlier on in the library I was sitting by the window feeling not good because I thought I probably wasn't going to be able to manage it. Then you came in and I thought – well, I thought, if we just go and do this birch swinging – well, who knows what might happen. And then, just now, seeing you hanging up there, that was it. God gave me the chance. That was the chance!"

"And you took it."

"Yes."

"And are you going to tell the others?"

"Yes. Yes, I think I am – or you can, if you don't mind – on Sunday."

By the time we arrived back at the house I found that my mood had shifted slightly. I managed to get my book in the end and my very hot bath and even my little rest in bed just as I had planned. The difference was that, for the first time in months, I thanked God for all those luxuries, and for some other very special things as well, things that I had lost, things that Peter would probably never have.

CHAPTER FIVE
Saturday Evening

S o, come on, Angela, tell us about your ghosts. Give us a bit of a scare!"

It was seven o'clock on Saturday evening. Remnants of a quaintly incongruous takeout dinner lay uncleared on the massive oak table in front of us. Mike had been the only one to have a very large meal at lunchtime, but this evening it didn't seem to have affected his appetite for Chinese food in the slightest. He was the one who had driven down to collect our order from the place in the village where I had stopped to read Angela's directions.

We were seated in what Angela referred to as the Banqueting Chamber in her publicity leaflets about the house, though I guessed that it had functioned as a spacious, elegantly proportioned drawing-room for most of its lengthy existence. In daylight hours an array of well-preserved leaded windows afforded wide views over more than an acre of overgrown, strikingly radiant green grass, the remains of what I imagined to have been an expansive and immaculate lawn in some distant age of unlimited cash and human resources. Nowadays the head gardeners and the under-gardeners and the gardeners' boys and whoever they had been allowed to kick no longer toiled to create an idyll for a handful of privileged people fancying the odd stroll or game of croquet on the front lawn. Perhaps their ghosts were here, but if so, they did no work. There was just deserted Angela, and a man she paid to bring his sit-on mower up from the village now and then to prevent the grass from getting completely out of control.

Now, of course, as we slumped in post-prandial repletion, apart from our own reflections nothing at all was visible through the tall, uncurtained windows, just the blackness of a cloud-laden, starless night and a very occasional isolated shock of splintered white light when a vehicle passed behind the bank of giant conifers that separated Angela's property from the public road leading to the village.

The bleakness of the afternoon had been dispelled, especially in this room. In the depths of the smoke-blackened chimney recess, spacious enough on its own to accommodate the six of us if we had desired to be that crazily intimate, yet another, much larger wood fire than the one in the kitchen sparkled and roared, its flames leaping like a male dancer. It needed to sparkle and roar. This house was huge, freezing, and unmanicured. Staying in it was the nearest I had got to camping out for quite a number of years. Both Jessica and I had always enjoyed camping, but neither of us had ever enjoyed the sensation of being cold.

The room was somnolently warm by the time we finished our meal and atmospheric beyond most places or experiences that I could remember. Apart from the roasting glow of the fire itself, the central section of the dining room was lit by the soft orange radiance emanating from a pair of brass paraffin lamps that had been set on opposite ends of the shelf above the fire, their tall glass chimneys narrowing like praying hands toward metal heat reflectors hanging from the high ceiling. Six candles set in wax-encased wine bottles of assorted shapes and sizes had been lit and placed by Angela at more or less regular intervals along the length of the dining-table.

As usual, these traditional, emotively simple sources of illumination had the interesting function of soothing and exciting soul and imagination at the same time. In addition, they obscured a hundred imperfections in us and in our surroundings. Light and shadow succeeded in turning the humblest object or artifact into a thing of beauty.

The far ends of the room and the lower part of the long paneled side wall opposite the fire were shrouded in a host of tumbling, quivering shadows, but at this particular moment the edges of this little world of ours mattered not a jot. We were in the center, we were warm (apart from my bath I was properly warm for the first time), and we were well fed. The faint odor of wax and paraffin merging with the subtle scents of Chinese food had made one or two of us a little thoughtful at first, but not for very long. The various dishes had been substantial and tasty. All that remained before us now was a polystyrene tub or two of that stuff no one ever puts on their food anyway and a litter of empty foil containers, scraped clean by Mike after the rest of us had indicated that we were defeated and could eat no more.

Conversation during dinner had tended to be light and inconsequential. Between Jenny and me a slight barrier had erected itself, presumably because of the intensive burst of mutual intimacy and revelation that had taken place up on top of the world. As far as I knew, no one else was aware of what had passed between us. Sitting opposite me now, she seemed to be having a little difficulty meeting my eyes. I wasn't doing very much better.

Around Graham, on the other hand, an almost visible aura of peace and catlike pleasure was beginning to form. Some inhibiting tension in him must have been eased. Possibly he had made a decision to appreciate – perhaps even to relish – the novelty and unpredictability of this weekend. Angela had been very kind and warm in all her dealings with him. That would have helped. That would have helped anyone. I frowned in disbelief at the thought of this Alan character upping and offing with his bimbo assistant. How could any sane man decide that it was a good idea to leave a woman like Angela?

Two glasses of wine in the course of his meal had painted a rosy smudge on each of Graham's cheeks, but it was not just the alcohol that was making his eyes shine and his mouth widen in that small smile of contentment as he stared into the fire or glanced up from time to time when someone spoke. For whatever reason, he was happy.

Next to me, and directly across the table from Graham, sat my birch-swinging companion, Peter. As usual, Peter had elected to drink water rather than wine, but perhaps God, in honor of what had happened this afternoon, had generously allowed a Cana-style miracle to transfigure the hydrogen and oxygen cocktail as it entered his carefully organized system, because he too seemed comfortably at peace this evening. Predictably, he had very little to say when our conversation was not focused on religion, but tonight, I said to myself, the persona of this man is manifesting itself in gentle curves instead of sharp right angles and symmetrical rhomboids. Could it have been the spirit of Jessica who, following this thought, whispered gently in my ear that a tendency to classify people in geometric terms is almost certainly an early sign of lunacy?

It was Mike, sitting with Graham and Peter on either side of him and facing Angela along the length of the table, who had asked the question about ghosts. Angela's magic – someone's magic, certainly not mine – must have done quite a bit of work on him as well, if not quite so successfully. Since the drama of last night he had regained his shape, but rather as a screwed-up sheet of paper regains its shape when you straighten it out. The creases were visible. Earlier in the day his renewed high spirits had had an air of feverish pleading about them, like a child who has been forgiven for some major wrongdoing and feels the need to expunge his debt to the grown-ups by contributing energetically to everything that's going on. That had largely faded now. Nevertheless, I thought, as I noted the way in which his spaniel eyes were fixed on Angela as he waited for her reply, having Mike here was rather like having a child with us. Two decades on, and he gave the impression of being no more fully formed as a personality than he had been when we knew him at St. Mark's. I found myself wondering if the conversation I had tried to start in the pub would ever be resumed.

"I don't mind. That's fine with me." Angela folded her arms, leaned them forward onto the table and looked from face to face. "We mustn't forget, though, that tonight we're scheduled to carry on sharing our greatest fears. We're not going to chicken out of that, are we?" She challenged us with her eyes. "Well, are we?"

Two little lines of worry disturbed the placidity of Graham's expression on being reminded of this prospect, but he moved his head slowly and definitely from side to side, as though, for him, that particular decision had been made and done and dusted long ago. Jenny carefully placed both hands flat on the table as she addressed Mike and then Angela.

"Forgive me, Mike, but I do have to say this – you are completely sure, Angela, that it's – well – safe to continue doing this thing about what we fear most? I'm only thinking that – I mean, it was so awful what happened with Andrew. Such terrible anger and hurt!" Her eyes, glistening with unshed tears in the flickering candlelight, seemed to me, irrelevant though the thought was, quite beautiful. "I was truly, truly shocked that all those horrible feelings could have been saved up and allowed to fester away for all those years, and then be dumped on poor Mike so cruelly. So, I was thinking, if there's any danger of anything at all like that happening again, it would be better if …"

Without finishing her sentence Jenny folded her outstretched hands into fists and crossed them self-consciously over her chest. Mike was studying his fingertips at the other end of the table. A protruding lower lip signaled the depth of concentration required for the task.

"I agree with Jenny." Angela sat back in her chair. She spoke with the kind of uncompromising frankness that is so useful in inspiring others. "I've got nothing negative to say about anyone who's here this weekend, and that's not why we're here anyway. The point – one of the points – isn't to tear the past and each other to bits but to find out where we are now compared with then. I'm a bit nervous about telling you what scares me most at the moment – certainly not ghosts, that's for sure – but this weekend is very important to me. And I really do want to know what's happened to you all since the old days. I honestly do. The idea of the fear thing was just to provide a sort of shortcut. We haven't got very long, after all, have we? So, before we go any further, is anyone else planning to do an Andrew on any of the rest of us, because, as Jenny's already said, that's not what we want."

There was a brief, classroom-like silence. Angela nodded once, firmly, before continuing.

"Good! No more heavy personal burdens from the past to be unloaded here, then – not ones that hurt others anyway."

I selected that moment to look up at Jenny, just as she happened to lift her eyes and look directly at me. We blushed like a pair of burning bookends, but as all of us were acquiring a fairly ruddy hue by then, I doubted that anyone else had noticed.

"So! You want to hear about one of my little ghosts before we start, do you? Is that unanimous, or is it just Mike who wants to be scared out of his tiny mind?"

"Yes, go on, Angela," said Graham, "I can't think of anything nicer than a good, spooky story to finish off our meal."

Jenny laughed at this, shrugging lightly to indicate her acquiescence in whatever the rest of us decided.

"We don't actually believe in ghosts, of course, and we would be most unwise to have anything to do with them," offered Peter matter-of-factly.

"We don't actually believe in ghosts, of course, and we'd be most unwise to have anything to do with them," mimicked Mike shrilly, his head on one side. "Oh, for goodness sake! Never mind what we don't believe in just for the minute." He reached across the table and made as if to baptize Peter's head with his own half-empty glass of water. "How are we supposed to have our hair stood on end by Angela if you're going to be reminding us every ten seconds that we don't believe in ghosts? Look, we're going to have a little ten-minute holiday from not believing in them. Then we'll repent. Okay? Tell you what – ask the famous Christian what he thinks."

I hated it when people did that to me, mainly because I had never had much more to say in any given area than anyone else. I just happened to say it in public. One of the problems I had discovered in the past about being a speaker on Christian subjects was that genuine protestations of inadequacy or uncertainty were sometimes disregarded. They were mere pebbles, skittering harmlessly about on the bedrock of my faith – that was what some of my wide-mouthed, baby-bird listeners wanted to believe.

Interestingly, there had been a faint worry about the whole ghost business in the back of my mind ever since I accepted Angela's invitation. Back in the good old St. Mark's days there had been a widespread if vague notion that masturbation, copyright violation, and pursuit of the occult were the three greatest sins known to humanity. Ghosts, as well as not existing, were bad things. It wasn't just a silly contradiction or paradox though. I had always believed that experimenting with darkness was bound to be destructive to the soul and the mind regardless of what existed and what did not. On the other hand, dealing or not dealing with Jessica's death had distracted me from the wearisome business of constantly policing myself. I felt the same as Graham tonight. A good shivery ghost story would just about touch the spot. Here we all were, satisfied and warm, sitting comfortably round this big old table together in the middle of a weekend that was orbiting around our real lives like a space capsule. Perhaps God would allow these two days to not count. I suspected that a stand-up comedian could not have got a better response from the hosts of heaven than I did with that last half-thought. I turned to Mike.

"Call me a famous Christian one more time, Mike," I said charmingly, "and regardless of your theology, you'll get that entire jug of water over you." Realizing the rashness of such a threat to such a personality, I continued hastily to our hostess, "Okay, Angela. Do your worst. If it gets too frightening we'll all sleep in here together in front of the fire tonight."

In fact, at that moment, in that situation, the idea of being very frightened by anything seemed little short of ridiculous. We tended to our own and each other's glasses (Jessica used to say that wine by candlelight is a poem that could only be destroyed by someone being foolish enough to write it), then turned expectantly toward Angela.

"Right," she said, resting her elbows on the table and placing the palms of her hands together as if she were about to pray, "I'll tell you a ghost story.

"First of all, I ought to come clean and say that I don't really know what to think about ghosts and ghouls. Things that go bump in the night so often turn out to be doors banging and things blown over by the wind, or foundations shifting, especially in this house. And then, of course, I've got a bit of a reputation to keep up for the visitors. When people come to look round one of the most haunted houses in England, they demand ghosts, and they've paid good money to have ghosts, so I make sure they get 'em! – well, I make sure they get stories about them anyway. Strangely warm beds on cold days, objects unaccountably moving from room to room, little girls in old-fashioned clothes seen walking across the lawn from upstairs windows at twilight – that sort of thing."

"You don't mean you make them up?"

Graham sounded more admiring than critical.

"Oh, no, they're actual tales that Alan and I were told by various people when we first came here. But they're all the sorts of stories that would come with any old common or garden haunted house if you were buying the complete set, if you know what I mean, and they were all things that happened to someone else, never to the person telling the story."

Mike picked up half a prawn cracker that had escaped his earlier attention. Narrowing his eyes and nibbling tiny pieces from the edge of it, he mumbled through the crumbs.

"So, you're saying there are no little ghosties."

Angela clasped her hands together on the table in front of her and, for the first time that evening, looked very serious.

"I'm going to tell you a story that I usually keep to myself. You'll see why when you hear it. I heard it only a month or so after coming here, and the person who told it to me is dead and gone, so I doubt if anyone else knows about it nowadays, not very accurately anyway." She broke off, frowning. "You are sure you want to hear this? It's – quite unpleasant in a way."

"Excellent!" said Mike.

Silent, rapt attention from the rest of us, an even more eloquent reply.

"Okay, as you wish. Well, as I said, we'd only been here a few weeks, and one day after doing a bit of shopping down in the village I decided to have a cup of coffee and read a newspaper in our one and only café, one of those really chintzy ones, in the High Street. I didn't get much reading done. The owner asked me where I was from and I told her that Alan and I had only recently bought Headly Manor. So we chatted for a bit and in the course of the conversation she mentioned that she knew a Doris Campbell who used to work up here three or four days a week, a long time ago, when it was owned by some posh people called Patterson. She's the one who said they were posh, by the way. Obviously thought I wasn't at all. I asked her what had happened to the Pattersons in the end, and she said, as far as she could remember, something strange and scary had happened, and the family had had a nasty accident one day not far from the house, and left not long after that, and it had all been a terrible shame, but she was sure she'd got a bit muddled about it, so why didn't I go round and ask Doris about it, because she knew all there was to know about it all, and she'd enjoy a bit of different company anyway."

"Mmm, shaping up nicely," commented Mike, rubbing his hands together in gleeful anticipation and adding in a silly, creepy Vincent Price voice, "Evil doings at the big house on the hill!"

"So," continued Angela, ignoring him, "as you can imagine I was pretty intrigued by this, and a possible true creepy story for the punters seemed a very good wheeze, so a couple of days later I dug out my portable tape recorder and took the trouble to track this Doris Campbell down to her council flat, which was up on what they call the Ridgeway, running along behind the police station just next to the little old-fashioned parade of shops where the post office is.

"Doris turned out to be Glaswegian and lovely. She was one of those overweight, kindly souls. Frilly blouse and heavy skirt. Happy eyes. Dead white permed hair. Rosy cheeks. Suffering terribly with her legs though. You know that awful swelling you see sometimes with older people when it seems to sort of overflow their shoes. She found it difficult just getting out of her chair, but that tiny little flat of hers was spotless, and she wouldn't hear of me making the tea when I got there. She had to do it. She really was very elderly and obviously not at all well. Dead lucid though. Bright as a button, and more than pleased to have an unexpected visitor, especially when she heard about the Manor connection. I told her that Alan and I had these plans to eventually open the place to the public, and in return she told me all about how she used to be the main one of what Mrs. Patterson called her 'ladies.' Did all sorts of different jobs at the big house. Cleaning, washing, even a bit of serving at table when special guests came to dinner. Apparently Mrs. Patterson 'trained her up properly' to make sure she laid the right number of knives and forks and handed everything out from the correct side and all that sort of thing.

"So, eventually I got round to asking her what had happened to the Pattersons in the end, and that was when she put her cup and saucer down and went very quiet, chewing her bottom lip and rocking to and fro for a little while as though she was trying to make a decision about something. Then she started speaking, but in a totally different way. If I wanted to accurately describe the way she spoke, I'd have to say that she was very – very grave.

"'Mrs. Steadman,' she said, 'you seem to me a very sensible, level-headed lady, so I'm going to tell you about something that happened up at the hall not long before Mr. and Mrs. Patterson and little Emily left – well, it was the main reason they left, although I think I must be the only one in the village who knows that. And I know what happened because I was there. I don't want you to feel you've got to worry, though, because it was a long time ago, and I've never heard or seen anything like it before or since up at the hall. But it was – it was very serious at the time. Very serious.'"

Angela paused dramatically. In the ensuing silence I prayed that Mike would not feel the need to sing the *X-Files* tune or suddenly reach out to grab Graham's arm and shout in his ear. Way above our heads the very faintest of scrabbling noises suggested the presence of mice or some other creature, probably up in one of the attics. Jenny momentarily lifted her gaze to the ceiling and shivered despite the heat of the fire.

"What happened?" Graham was totally caught up in the story.

"Well, this is the way Doris told it to me," continued Angela. "It was one day in late autumn, this time of year, in fact, about six-thirty in the evening. Mr. Patterson was due home from his rich-making, high-powered work in the city in about half an hour, and Mrs. Patterson was busy in the kitchen – which I don't think can have been so very different from the way it is now – getting a meal ready for the four of them, including Doris, who'd been hoovering right through the house all afternoon.

"Little Emily Patterson was seven years old at the time. She was a bright, happy, intelligent kid according to Doris. She'd been decanted a few minutes earlier by the parent of a school friend after some kind of after-school thing. Apparently Emily and Doris got on like a house on fire, and no more than a few minutes after arriving home, Emily, who'd rushed in all excited, shedding bits of her day left, right, and center, asked Doris if she'd come up to her bedroom while she got changed so that she could tell her all about being given a part in some play that evening.

"Doris said that so far this was all quite normal and unexceptional.

"So, the two of them climbed the back stairs, the ones that eventually lead up to the room you're in, David. Emily was a bit in front of Doris, having scampered up the stairs like a demented rabbit, I expect, the way children do, and was about to turn right toward her bedroom at the end of the landing when she seemed to stop dead, as though her eye had been caught by something along to the left. Then she actually moved off in that direction and disappeared from sight.

"When Doris finally puffed her way to the top, she found the little girl a few yards along the landing, head back, peering up into a dark rectangular hole that opened into one of the attics when its wooden hatch was moved aside, as was the case now. Emily was standing with one foot on the bottom rung of a stepladder that stood directly under this opening, staring into the black space with eyes as round as portholes, probably enjoying a few goosebumps at the thought of that dark, cobwebby place up there above her head.

"Now, Doris was quite surprised to see the ladder there. She knew Mrs. Patterson had been up in the loft earlier that day stowing away a box of unwanted bits and pieces, but she could have sworn the ladder had been replaced in its cupboard just along the landing afterward. She was much more surprised to see the hatch left open. Mrs. Patterson and her husband had a real horror of their beloved daughter getting accidentally hurt in the house – especially this house, because of the whole place being sort of creaky and unpredictable. For Mrs. Patterson to leave that hatch open with a ladder standing underneath it at a time when Emily was due home from school at any minute was so out of character as to seem virtually impossible.

"We stretch the muscles of our credulity to accommodate things we don't understand, though, don't we? And that's exactly what Doris did on this occasion. She assumed that either Mrs. Patterson had some good but as yet unexplained reason for leaving things in that state, or it was maybe one of those lapses in concentration that we're all guilty of from time to time. Putting it out of her mind for the time being, but thinking she'd mention it to her employer when they got back downstairs, she hustled the little girl away from the ladder and back along the landing past the top of the stairs to her bedroom at the other end of the passage, the one Andrew slept in last night. For the next few minutes or so she sat on the bed listening to Emily prattling happily on about her drama group and her school day and what her friends were up to. Doris was just beginning to think they ought to be heading downstairs again when both of them heard Mrs. Patterson's voice calling faintly but audibly from somewhere beyond the closed bedroom door.

"'Emily! Emily, darling, do you want to come up and see what mummy found in the loft today?'

"Naturally, Emily got wildly excited about doing something so deliciously frightening and safe, and started squealing, 'Mummy's letting me go up in the loft with her! Mummy's letting me go up in the loft with her!'

"Half in and half out of a jumper, she pulled the door open and, closely followed by Doris, happily convinced now that the loft mystery was more or less solved, started toward the ladder at the other end of the landing. Doris said (and Emily said exactly the same later on) that she could see, as clearly as you like, Mrs. Patterson's slim, bare arm reaching down from the hole in the ceiling. Without giving it any particular thought at the time, she even found herself noticing the familiar solitaire diamond wedding ring on the third finger of the hand that was waiting to help Emily up from the ladder into the attic.

"Doris said that what happened in the next few seconds was like one of those dreams where everything happens in slow motion and you don't think you're going to be able to move fast enough to do the thing that'll avoid a frightful disaster.

"Emily was no more than a step or two away from the bottom of the ladder at the moment when Doris passed the top of the flight of stairs that the two of them had come up a little earlier. At that precise second Doris happened to glance down to her left. What she saw there filled her with such horror and confusion that for a split second she did nothing at all. Standing just on the bend of the stairs, looking up inquiringly toward Doris, was Emily's mother, Mrs. Patterson.

"Doris said she felt as if her brain had slowed down like a record played at the wrong speed, and her body had ceased to function. Simply turning her head again seemed to take a huge effort, as though she was straining at some horribly heavy weight. The sight that met her eyes when she did manage it stuck in her memory for the rest of her life, like a photograph you don't want to look at but you can't throw away or destroy. Emily's left foot was actually on the bottom rung of the ladder, her hand extended trustingly upward to grasp the larger hand that still stretched down welcomingly from the darkness of the loft. It was another paralyzed fraction of a second before Doris was able to locate the muscles of her mouth and make them work. Then she gathered all her terror and apprehension into one shouting, screaming cry of warning:

"'EMILY! NO!'

"Emily jumped as if she'd been shot, and after one confused, fleeting look upward, flung herself, white-faced, along the landing toward Doris, who grabbed her and bundled her down the stairs past her bewildered mother, who followed them, of course, back down to the lower part of the house. The two of them sat on the sofa in the kitchen crying their eyes out, Doris because something horribly inexplicable and dangerous had happened, Emily because she had no idea what was going on and she'd been badly frightened by Doris screaming so loudly at her. She thought she must have done something terribly naughty, you see."

Angela sat back in her chair and glanced around at our faces. She certainly had our full attention. Mike was the first to speak. He sounded like someone who has found the last page of his whodunit missing.

"And? So? What happened?"

"What do you mean?"

"Well, you know, when they went back upstairs – When did they go back upstairs? What did they find?"

"Oh, right. Well, Mr. Patterson turned up just after that, and when he heard what had happened he grabbed a golf club and went to have a look. When he came back down he said he couldn't understand what they were talking about, because he'd found the hatch closed and the ladder back in its cupboard. Apparently he actually lugged the ladder out for himself and climbed right up into the loft – "

"Goodness me, that was very brave!" said Jenny. "I don't think anything could have persuaded me to go up there, especially on my own. Did he – did he find anything?"

"Nothing unusual or out of place. Certainly no red-faced ghouls or ghosts. They calmed Emily down as best they could and plonked her in front of the television, and then the Pattersons and Doris sat down with a shot of brandy each and went over and over what had happened. Mrs. Patterson explained that she'd come up the stairs because she thought she heard someone shouting out. Doris reckoned that could only have been the voice that called from the loft, the same one that had brought her and Emily along the landing."

"And what about Emily?" I asked. "Was she very upset by it all – in the long term, I mean?"

"No, not really. Doris said that with everything happening so fast, she'd barely registered the fact that her mother seemed to be in two places at the same time. She'd been more upset by being shouted at, and when Doris told her something about being worried that she'd fall off the ladder and hurt herself she quite happily accepted it. Kids of that age do, don't they? Well, the ones who've never had any reason to stop trusting the grown-ups do, anyway."

"And the parents?"

"Ah, that was different, I'm afraid. Mr. Patterson was just a bit skeptical at first. You could hardly blame him. But when he added together the things that Doris and Emily said, and the fact that his wife had also heard this voice calling out, well, that's when the trouble really started. Because, whatever this thing was – and obviously no one could quite say what it was – if it had nearly happened once, then it could actually happen again. And the person it had nearly happened to was their beloved Emily. They made sure she slept in their bedroom from that night onward, and she was never allowed to go up the stairs on her own again.

"Doris said the worry over that one incident just wore them down after a while, the constant fear that, however silly it might sound to outsiders, someone – something – might be waiting for a chance to get Emily. They felt as if they were going mad. To cut a long story short, in the end they decided to get out. It all happened very quickly after that. When the lorry had gone on their moving day they put a few last odds and ends in their estate car and drove up to the end of the drive, and there, for some unknown reason that he never could explain, Mr. Patterson pulled out into the lane without stopping or looking. A Land Rover coming down the lane toward the village went straight into them – hit the back door and buckled it in to within inches of where the little girl was sitting. She wasn't hurt, a bit shaken up, but ..."

"But they thought it was this evil something-or-other having one last go at Emily?"

"I suppose so. I think so. That's the way Doris told it to me, Graham. Apparently they didn't even go back to the house after the accident. They just walked down into the village to Doris's house and fixed things up from there."

Silence. This all seemed a very long way from strangely warmed beds or objects moving from room to room or even harmless old Cavaliers statutorily carrying their severed heads along battlements.

Before speaking again Graham glanced around the table as if he thought that someone else might have been about to make a comment. Nobody did.

"And nothing like that's happened since?"

"Not to my knowledge. Definitely not to me. I sometimes wonder if ghosts are like dogs."

I was happy to supply the cue.

"Because ...?"

"Because I have a distinct feeling they're far less likely to be aggressive with people who aren't scared of them."

Graham took the tiniest of sips from his glass of wine as he pondered for a moment or two.

"I was just wondering," he said, "if anyone asked Emily what she saw when she looked up into the attic, the second time I mean, just before Doris shouted at her. What I mean is – well, was there anything on the other end of the arm?"

There was something horribly bald about the way in which Graham had phrased his question. I shivered a little myself at the realization that my own bedroom was a matter of feet away from the site of such strange, inexplicable happenings. Jessica and I had never really discussed such things. Our shoulder imps had never let us. We never would now. The familiar wave of alienation and childlike rage swept through me at the notion of my wife going off to qualify for after-death experiences and failing to take me with her. Oh, Jessica, Jessica, Jessica! Please don't be dead …

"Actually they did," said Angela, answering Graham's question, "but all she could or possibly would say was that 'mummy's arm came out of the black.'"

"And into the red," was Mike's annoyingly meaningless attempt at a witty rejoinder.

Angela smiled generously. "Actually, Mike, that's not so very far off the truth. Selling up so quickly and unexpectedly probably did put the poor old Pattersons solidly in the red, just like me now. Speaking of which, what I could do with is discovering a spot of treasure trove or a few doubloons hidden around the place. I suppose none of you have become incredibly rich, have you?"

Peter stirred his angular body on his chair as though he was trying to unstick it.

"I think the whole thing sounds thoroughly satanic and dreadful," he said worriedly. "If it had been me, Angela, I would have gone round and prayed in every room and corridor in the house after hearing that awful story. I really would."

"We did exactly that, Peter," replied Angela quietly, the firm lines of her personality fading and losing their power of direction before our eyes for the first time since the beginning of the weekend. "Alan and I prayed in every room and in all three of the attics and most of the outhouses. We prayed for the people who'd used them and lived in them over the centuries, and for all the people who were going to visit and enjoy them when we got the place up and running. Every night after dinner we prayed for ourselves and our marriage and our future and the children we might have. We prayed a lot. It was exciting. It was part of being us. I was stupidly happy – stupidly happy."

A slight unease fluttered our spirits. Not so good. It was like your mum being ill. Get better soon, Angela, so that you can look after us all.

"What I do think remarkable, Angela," said Jenny, carefully dispassionate, "is that you were able to go on living here at all after hearing that story. You had to go along that landing every day, I expect?" Angela nodded. "And sometimes even go up into that very same loft." Screwing her eyes tight shut. "I know I couldn't have done that. I know I couldn't." She glanced briefly and nervously over her left and then her right shoulder. "It's bad enough thinking of going up to bed tonight, let alone living here on my … well, er, you ended up on your own, didn't you? Oh, dear, please forgive me. I set out to change the subject and ended up working my way round to the place where I didn't want to be." With an embarrassed glance at me: "Why am I so good at putting my foot in it? That's the second time this weekend. I can't believe it. I am such a twit!"

Seeing the purple confusion that accompanied the conclusion of this well-meant speech, Angela reached out and patted Jenny's hand. Her smile switched itself on once more, kind and reassuring, making her strong again. I sighed, as imperceptibly as possible, wondering what it would be like to kiss Angela full on her warm, soft mouth. A picture of her profile and the side of her face as she sat in front of me next to Jessica in the group all those years ago flashed to the front of my mind. I breathed deeply and abandoned my speculation, just as I had often done in those days.

Angela spoke reassuringly, "You're no such thing, Jenny, I promise you. I know perfectly well you were rescuing me, you twit. Oh, no! You've got me doing it now!" Everyone laughed comfortably. "In any case, if we're going to talk about twits, then we might as well talk about me. My brain's been falling apart lately. You would not believe what I did the other day! Just listen to this, everybody."

Angela gestured with open hands to include us all.

"I went to see a friend of mine over between Stroud and Gloucester because I needed a bit of practical advice on business strategy, right? Quite important stuff. Okay, so I'm sitting opposite my friend at her kitchen table, and when the right moment comes I lean forward, very intense and serious, her eyes and mine locked together and all that, and I say, 'Look – Rachel, what I really want you to do, if it's okay, is to let me pick your nose.' "

We all burst into laughter. Mike nearly expired. Angela flapped a hand, begging to be allowed to finish her story.

"Listen! Listen! Poor Rachel went on looking into my eyes for what seemed like an awful long time, and then she said, very slowly and with a sort of edgy, ready-to-run wariness, 'Angela, I really am praying very hard indeed that you meant to say "my brains." For one horrible second, I'm sure the poor girl was terrified that I was inviting her to become my partner in some brand-new, sad little perversion. So – Jenny, twit me no twits. I am the champion!"

I let the laughter subside to nearly nothing before I said, "So, losing Alan was worse than any ghostly encounter?"

Angela had been in the process of tilting a half-full wine bottle toward her glass. At my words she froze for an instant, then very slowly returned it to an upright position, placing it back on the table with meticulous care. When she did look up at me at last her gaze was calmly challenging.

"I hope you're as ready to answer questions like that as you are to ask them, David."

"I ... well, you'd better talk to Jenny about that."

"What? Oh!" Jenny clicked into comprehension with a little start.

ADRIAN PLASS

"Yes, well, that's right. Up on the hills today I, er, I told David how desperately in love with him I used to be at St. Mark's, and he told me – "

"I'll tell you who I fancied!" Jenny's constructive bridging exercise was crudely interrupted by Mike's loud voice. He had clearly found this fresh subject, one that Jenny must have hoped would flitter quickly by like an anonymous little brown bird, very much to his taste. "Anyone remember the name of that girl from Becket Memorial who only came for a while?" He clicked his fingers twice in frustration. "You know! Long black hair, confident type, never quite learned the lingo. Fabulous chest."

"Her name was Amanda Nichols," supplied Graham, adding pinkly after a minuscule delay, "Yes, you're right, she did have very long black hair."

"She never made a commitment as such," said Peter sadly, "but I seem to remember she came very close."

"She definitely came very close to me," hooted Mike raucously. "Hands up who remembers that youth weekend they took us on down in Dorset one year, when we stayed at some kind of posho girls' boarding school in the middle of nowhere."

"Everyone here was definitely there," asserted Peter confidently, looking and sounding rather like a Tenniel character from *Alice in Wonderland* as he bobbed a knuckle toward each of us in turn as though he was counting.

"Anyway, this girl – "

"Oh, I remember that weekend." Jenny's smile was rueful. "There were about eight of us girls sleeping in a sort of dormitory place, and after we'd woken up on the first morning we all got our Bibles and notebooks out like good little Christian girls, and I felt guilty because, although I did pray and read the Bible quite a lot, I didn't always have a quiet-time in the morning at home, and I thought all the others probably did, but I didn't want them to know. How silly! I don't suppose half of them did either."

"Amanda and I went – "

"Well, I didn't for one," said Angela, "and I'm pretty sure I was in the same room as you. Now I come to think of it, nor did – nor did the girl in the bed next to me. She told me she didn't. Funny. I'd forgotten all that. It matters a lot at that age, doesn't it, what other people think. But – "

"Jessica, you're talking about?"

"Jessica, that's right, David, yes."

Linking my fingers behind my head, I tilted my chair back on two legs, physically retreating from what I was about to say. "Look, please can I just make it clear, everyone, you don't have to leave Jessica's name out of the conversation because I happen to be sitting here. She wouldn't want that and neither would I. Okay? I really don't mind her being talked about. Well, I do. I mean, I did. But I don't. Oh, dear! I don't know what I'm talking about – "

A truly blessed, entirely unexpected guffaw of laughter escaped me at this juncture. Despite everything, another striking aspect of that church weekend in Dorset had bounced abruptly to the surface of my memory. I swung my chair forward on all four legs with a bump.

"Hey! Remember the six-inch rule and all the bother that caused?"

This sparked off a general hubbub of laughter and reminiscence. I had guessed it probably would. The infamous six-inch rule had been devised by Malcolm, our curate leader, and Ethel, his assistant (not in the same room together without anyone else present, of course) presumably to ensure that no "hanky-panky" blotted the escutcheon of our church youth weekend. To be fair, their motivation may have been on a slightly higher level than that. Possibly the idea was simply to prevent the general loss of cohesion that might have resulted from couples winding themselves round each other on the periphery of the main group. Or perhaps they just wanted to avoid unnecessary distractions from the spiritual content of the weekend. Whatever the truth actually was, this rule, stipulating that boys and girls must not, at any time during the weekend, allow themselves to come within less than six inches of each other, led to nothing but trouble.

Apart from anything else, it was somehow typical of those who concern themselves with the sexual morality of the young that they should have (quite innocently on a conscious level, I'm sure) elected the sacred measurement of six inches to be a suitable distance for couples to maintain. Ribald jokes on the subject abounded among less reverent members of the St. Mark's male contingent, particularly as we were all at an age when the size of our genitalia was what St. Paul might have described as a burning issue.

The main problem, though, was that the first evening and the following morning of the weekend were dogged, as far as poor Malcolm and Ethel were concerned, by the punishingly visible, bonelessly limp depression of a handful of heartbroken couples, tragically pining for each other on opposite sides of the room where we all met to be inspired as a group. Quite honestly, this cast a much greater sense of gloom and disunity over the proceedings than if each of the couples in question had spent the whole weekend in a sleeping-bag on one of the dining room tables. It all got sorted out in the end somehow, but a very great deal of time was wasted.

At that stage Jessica and I weren't yet going out together. I never dared say so at the time, but I would have cheerfully settled for being allowed to spend the whole weekend at a distance of six inches from her.

There was a lull. Mike tried again.

"One night this girl and I — "

"Wasn't there something about a hummingbird?" asked Graham, by now in a state of blissful relaxation. He seemed hardly able to contain his pleasure at being part of all this drinking and talking and laughing and remembering.

"The speaker!" Looking more like Beardsley than ever, Peter sat rigidly upright, that knuckle of his uncurling into a bony finger on the end of a quivering, outstretched arm, pointing in Graham's direction as though he had solved some great mystery of the universe. "He told us we shouldn't be like South American hummingbirds!"

"Eh? What?" Momentarily distracted from his story by this extraordinary comment, Mike frowned and rubbed his eyes. "What do you mean he said we shouldn't be like hummingbirds? What's that all about? Don't smoke, don't drink, don't go with women, and, whatever you do, folks, don't ever make the mistake of sucking nectar from flowers while you're flying backward. Can't say I remember that one."

"It was the man who came to speak to us during the weekend," said Peter. A succession of memories illuminated his face like lights being switched on one by one in a dark church hall. "He came on Friday evening, and he had a brown leather briefcase, and he did a short talk in the getting-to-know-each-other slot after dinner to say that his sessions were going to be on the subject of 'Love Your Neighbor', and – "

"And he was very tall with red hair and he blinked a lot," added Angela, apparently infected with the general fever of recollection.

"But what was this thing about the hummingbirds?" asked Jenny when the noise had died down. "That wasn't made up, was it? I think I can just about remember him mentioning something like that, but I don't have a clue what it was. Hummingbirds?"

"It was quite a good point he made, actually," said Peter with judicious earnestness.

Friendly groans from most of us. We're gaining in confidence, I thought to myself. Safe and warm with each other – for this evening at least. All at once, unnervingly, for the first time since her sad, sad death, I wanted more than anything else in the world to talk to these people about my Jessica. Now. But it wasn't my turn. Not yet. Would I still want the same thing later on?

"I remember what it was now," announced Graham triumphantly, tapping rhythmically on the edge of the table with one side of his finger. "He said that most of us are very selfish and only think about ourselves, and he said that it was important for we young

Christian people not to be like a hummingbird that he'd personally seen during a missionary trip to South America."

"Yes!" raved Mike wildly, balling his fists and grinding the words out through his teeth, "but we want to know why not! Please tell us! What appalling, dreadful, evil thing do these sodding little birds do?"

"He said," explained Graham, in a triumph of recollection, moving his outstretched hand through the air as he spoke, presumably to mimic the flight of a hummingbird, "that as they fly along, they go, 'ME-ME-ME-ME-ME-ME-ME-ME-ME-ME-ME-ME-ME!'"

So, where were we?"

"Well," I replied to Angela, "let me see now. You were avoiding talking about Alan and I was avoiding talking about Jessica. Jenny tried to help by starting to talk about what happened up on the hills today but was interrupted by Mike, who was doing his best to tell us about some teenage sex romp with what's-her-name – Amanda Nichols – but never did get round to it, partly because we really didn't want to hear it, but mostly because we got on to the subject of the six-inch rule and the man who told us we shouldn't be like hummingbirds. Is that about it?"

My little summary was greeted with laughter and a spontaneous patter of applause from the others. We seemed to have successfully transferred our newfound atmosphere of warmth and togetherness from the dining room to the kitchen, where, thanks to energetic efforts by Mike in his cooperative mode much earlier in the day, and acting under strict orders from the lady of the house, another blazing log fire awaited us.

"No alcohol" was Angela's arbitrary rule for this part of Saturday evening, and probably a wise one if people were genuinely intending to talk about things that were important to them. The belief that alcohol improves performance is, for most people, as deluded in relation to conversation as it is in relation to driving or sex. On the low table before us stood two tall cafetières of strong coffee next to milk, sugar, and a bowl containing the less popular remnants of Jenny's chocolates. We had all helped ourselves to both before settling back into the sofa and four deep armchairs that made up the sitting room end of Angela's long kitchen. Much as I agreed with the "no alcohol" dictum, I couldn't help reflecting on the fact that not so much as a drop of wine had passed Andrew's lips in advance of his calculated attack on Mike last night. Perhaps, I thought, it would have been better if he had downed a glass or two. One brief little bank holiday would surely have done him no harm at all.

"Come on, then, Mike," said Angela, "if you really must get it off your chest, tell us what happened with Amanda Nichols. But we insist you keep it either clean or interesting."

Mike was comfortably ensconced on the sofa beside Jenny, sitting, in fact, exactly where Andrew had sat the night before.

"Ah, well, yes." He did a slightly unpleasant, relish-filled wriggle into his corner of the sofa. "Yes, you see, Amanda got it into her head that she and I should slip out on the Saturday night and go for a swim in that big pond down behind the trees at the bottom of the field at the back. Remember the pond? So I told her that was all very fine as an idea, but I hadn't got any swimming things. And she said she hadn't either, but there was no reason for that to be a problem, was there? Well, I mean – I just goggled at her! Thought for a minute she meant we'd swim in our clothes. Then I saw the way she was looking at me and it clicked. Wow! My first time coming up. It's a good job no one else was in my head for the rest of that day, I can tell you. Eat your heart out, you sad little hummingbirds."

"Are you seriously saying that this happened during the St. Mark's youth weekend?" Peter's eyes bulged as if someone was inflating them from behind with a bicycle pump. "What if Malcolm and Ethel had found out?"

Clearly, the idea of "Malcolm and Ethel finding out" invoked as much spine-tingling horror in Peter today, now that he was in his thirties, as it had done when he was a lad of sixteen or seventeen.

"I expect they'd have joined us," replied Mike flippantly. "They'd have probably said it's perfectly all right to swim together in the nude as long as someone else is there at the same time – all right, all right, you can put your jaws together again, Pete, me old mate. That was just a joke. You're right. They'd have gone raving mad and sent us home – and then forgiven us after a decent interval."

"So, did you go?" Graham sounded slightly hoarse.

"Did I? Wouldn't you have gone?"

"Well, I'm not sure ..."

I felt absolutely sure that Graham would not have gone. I was fairly sure that he would have wished he had afterward.

"Course I did. Of course I went. I've never forgotten it. Lovely warm, moonlit night, it was. We met up by the kitchen door round the back of the house with our towels and crept along behind the hedge that ran down the hill toward the bottom gate. When we got down behind the trees she didn't waste any words, just dropped her towel on the ground, stripped off, quick as a blink because she'd left all her undies off, and dived in. So I did the same. When we came out she dried herself on her towel and then just laid on her back on the grass staring up at the sky, with not a stitch on, all lit up by the moon. What a body! Soft and silvery."

Mike took a deep breath, lost in reverie for a moment.

"Then she asked me if I wanted to do it with her."

A great stillness had settled on the rest of us. I cleared my throat.

"And did you?"

"Did I want to, you mean?"

"No, you twit! Did you do it?"

A suggestive leer crept on to Mike's face. He opened his mouth to speak.

"We girls do talk, you know, Mike," interposed Angela casually, as she popped a chocolate into her mouth. "As a matter of fact, as you were speaking I suddenly remembered Amanda telling me about this, although at the time she refused to say who it was, even when I hit her with a pillow. She just said it was one of the boys."

Mike pursed his lips, then chewed on a fingernail as he peered intently at Angela, brows furrowed. He was trying to see right inside her head.

"No," he said gruffly at last, "wanted to, but – I couldn't." He glanced at Angela again and sighed. "When I thought of all the times I'd sat in a café with some girl, dreaming about what I'd like to do to her, and then made a complete fool of myself by having to make idiotic, stupid excuses for not standing up when it was time to go – it's all right for you women. And then when it actually came to it, I dunno. I was a flop. Literally. I think she was a bit too – "

"Too much in charge?" suggested Angela, with just the faintest trace of bitterness in her voice. "The pencil-sharpener more impressive than the pencil?"

"Something like that, I suppose." He shifted in his seat, wrestling with the memory. "You know, I couldn't believe she was just lying there, starkers, waiting for me to do what I'd been thinking about doing all day, or for two or three years, depending how you look at it. I'll tell you what I reckon it was. I don't think I'd twigged that women's bodies were so – well, so real, all made of flesh and skin and hair and stuff. Blimey! What am I going on about? Actually – maybe it was the moonlight. Made it all a bit too much like a fairytale. Sex and fairytales don't really go together, do they?"

"No," said Angela.

"And how did Amanda react to your, er – your lack of interest?" asked Jenny.

Mike turned to her, raised his eyebrows, and shrugged. "Didn't seem that bothered either way, to be honest. Certainly didn't make a fuss about it anyway. She had another swim, then we got dressed and went back up to the house. She must have gone back to her room – fell fast asleep I expect, and I went back to mine and spent what you might call a restless night, to put it mildly, wishing I could have another go and hoping she wasn't going to tell anyone." He looked quizzically at Angela. "I'm quite surprised she talked about it really. Are you sure she didn't say who it was?"

"She didn't say anything at all about it," confessed Angela serenely. "I made that up to ensure we got the strictly historical version, rather than the one you've been regaling your mates with for goodness knows how long. I hadn't the faintest idea whether you'd actually 'done it' or not."

Mike stared at her blankly as his brain computed this piece of information. At last a wry smile appeared on his face. Once again grudging admiration had succeeded in chasing away the potential affront.

"Well, you're right," he said, "I suppose I have sort of told it the way I wished it'd been." Something seemed to strike him forcibly. "In fact, it had gotten so I really did remember her and me having sex three times in the moonlight. But – we didn't, did we?" He slumped back in his seat, saucer-eyed, like a puzzled small child. "You know, I can't believe that's not true. It wasn't my first time after all, was it? I made it up."

"Yes, but what amazes me" – Peter was on the point of bursting – "is that two members of a church youth group should even contemplate going off at night to have – well, to do that sort of thing. We weren't supposed to be even thinking about sex."

"Well, at least Amanda and I were following our instincts a bit and having an adventure," declared Mike, apparently revived by Peter's outburst, "while you lot were telling yourselves sex didn't exist and pretending to be spiritual. At least we were honest."

"Oh, really, that is so silly!" Jenny bent forward and banged her empty mug down on the table exasperatedly. Her accent seemed to grow stronger and stronger as she continued to speak. "I'm sorry, but this is exactly the sort of thing that makes it so difficult for young Christians, or ancient Christians or Christians of any age for that matter, to get the whole business of sex into perspective. Let's face it, we all – nearly all of us, anyway – want to have sex." She challenged us with her eyes. It appeared that none of us were willing to take up the challenge. "We want to have sex with the right people and the wrong people, in appropriate situations and in inappropriate ones. When I was on that church weekend I'm quite sure my head was full of sex. I thought about it and dreamed about it and sometimes pictured having the most lurid experiences you can imagine with the sort of people Malcolm and Ethel and my mother would definitely not have wanted me to go around with. I'm pretty sure some of my fantasies would have made Mike's fairytale moonlight encounter beside the bloody pond look as pure as the driven snow."

She drew breath for a moment.

"No, Peter, I didn't go on that weekend to think about sex, any more or less than I went on that weekend to not think about sex. I went there to be who I am and, hopefully, to let that person meet God and find out what he wanted to say to me. I wasn't interested in what he wanted to say to some weird, cleaned-up version of me, but to the incomplete, complex, sinful person that I actually was – still am."

Seeing Jenny's head turn in his direction, and sensing that her guns were about to be turned on him, Mike flamboyantly pressed himself even farther back into his corner of the sofa.

"As for you, Michael Ford, you know how much I hated what Andrew did last night, but you've just done precisely what he accused you of, and you can't be allowed to get away with it. I can assure you that at no stage did I tell myself sex didn't exist, nor did I, except for the silly quiet-time, reading your Bible thing, knowingly pretend to be spiritual. In the highly unlikely event that some boy had invited me to go bathing in the nude at midnight with the option of making mad passionate love afterward, I would probably have wanted to go very much – depending on who'd invited me, I hasten to add. But I'm pretty sure that, in the end, I wouldn't have gone. Partly because of fear and lack of confidence, I don't mind admitting that, but mainly because it really, really did matter to me that, as far as I'd worked it out, and I have to tell you I don't give twopence for how other people work it out, God wanted me to stay a virgin until I got married. I'm still a virgin for that same reason. I do my very best not to indulge them, but I still have all sorts of fantasies about screwing with all sorts of people, and I shall continue to follow Jesus in this state until either he finds a man for me to marry, or I die, in which case it won't be an issue any more. What he wants is more important to me than anything else.

"Is all that honest enough for you? Believe it or not, Mike, there's more than one kind of adventure in this world, and I am not celibate by some sort of stupid, wimpish default. Have I made myself clear?"

Mike grimaced, nodding rapidly and defensively, temporarily cowed by this shrapnel burst of words. With her cheeks flaming and her eyes flashing, Jenny looked as vibrant and alive now as she had done up on the hills this morning. I wondered if anyone would ever get round to researching the correlation between spirituality and sex appeal. Not a question to be raised just at the moment. What a woman she was revealing herself to be. And what a Christian. Her words had stirred something in me for the first time in months. It had been like listening to the sound of a trumpet. I was almost beginning to feel excited about the idea of getting back on a platform again – almost.

"So – do you mean to say that lust is all right, then?" asked Graham, who had listened to every word of Mike's account and Jenny's impassioned speech with total absorption.

"I think what Jenny's saying is that regardless of whether it's all right or not, it happens. But the thing is, Graham," Angela screwed her eyes tight shut and clicked her tongue with frustration, "asking if it's 'all right' doesn't really get us where we want to be, does it? It makes us sound like twerpy kids in an infant class checking nervously with each other about what might make teacher cross. We might not know much, but I think we have to deal with what we do know in as grown-up a way as possible."

Levering herself out of her chair and dropping to her knees beside the fire, Angela took a couple of birch logs from the wicker basket that stood against the wall. Averting her face to avoid the intense heat, she leaned forward and half-dropped, half-threw them carefully into the very center of the blaze before sitting back on her heels. What a waste of valuable silver, I thought.

"Jesus said that just lusting after someone in your heart means you've already committed adultery, so there you are. It's not 'all right.' But nor is talking nonsense about the difficulties that arise – or in Mike and Amanda's case didn't – when you try to honestly take that on board. Covering it up is like putting those silly woolly whatsits over your spare toilet rolls. Mind you," her hands dropped helplessly to her sides in a little moment of desolation, "Jesus also made it perfectly clear that we mustn't condemn people who are guilty of adultery, so I guess I've been failing pretty badly on both counts lately. There's murder in my heart, folks. I can't stop hating. Haven't given up yet though."

She looked so sad kneeling there. At once Jenny left her seat without a word, knelt down in front of Angela, and gathered her into an embrace.

Jessica and I had often expressed our disquiet about certain exponents and advocates of the modern hugging culture, especially in the so-called family of the church. I, especially, found it extremely difficult to offer or receive "hugs without history," as we privately called them. But what Jenny had done was just about as right as it could be. I had always thought that women tended to be better at this sort of thing than men. They didn't seem to feel the need to indulge in the mutual back-patting that most of us manly blokes used to cover our embarrassment. Jessica said that when men hugged they looked as if they were trying to bring up each other's wind.

Hug over, Angela dried her eyes on a tissue pulled from the sleeve of her jumper. After a grateful little smile to Jenny, who was dabbing at her own eyes as she settled back into her chair, she turned to Mike. Damage limitation, I guessed. I was right. Good old Angela.

"I was just thinking, Mike," she said, with a sort of rainbow brightness, "I bet you made up for this moonlight disaster of yours later on. Am I right?"

"Not half," agreed Mike in somewhat thin buccaneering style, and then, with a strange depth of sadness, "none of 'em as good as the first time, though, when I didn't actually do it – three times."

You know who we really need here, don't you?" said Angela a few minutes later when mugs had been refilled and spirits restored a little. "I should have asked Malcolm and Ethel to come down. They'd have put us back on the straight and narrow. None of this flying off at tangents if they'd been here. I wonder what they would have made of Mike's little escapade. Come on, we're allowed a one-word guess each. Fire at will."

"Deeply shocked?" suggested Peter in a slightly troubled voice.

"That's two words," said Jenny. "Amazed, I would say."

"I suspect that their flabbers would have been completely gasted," said Mike lazily.

I said, "That's lots of words, but I suppose it's based on one word so we'll let you off." I thought for a moment. "They would have been discombobulated."

Getting up and moving round to the space behind the sofa as we spoke, Angela had taken a heavy volume down from one of the shelves that lined the wall at the end of the room. Resuming her seat, she flicked through the pages for a second or two before finding what she was looking for.

"Here we are. I think they would have been 'agitated, appalled, astounded, confounded, disgusted, dismayed, disquieted, horrified, jarred, jolted, nauseated, numbed, offended, outraged, paralyzed, revolted, scandalized, shaken, sickened, staggered, startled, stunned, stupefied, traumatized, unnerved, and unsettled.' "

She slapped the book shut triumphantly.

"A bit hurt?" said Graham quietly.

A faintly shame-scented silence.

"Anyway," Angela laid the thesaurus gently down on the floor beside her chair, "in their honor, let's get ourselves a bit more organized. What do we fear most? That's the question we said we'd answer."

"Miss! Miss! Done mine, Miss!" cried Mike, leaning forward and waving his arm stiffly in the air like a keen infant.

"Mm. Andrew's done his as well. Five left. I gather Peter's asked if he can do his at communion in the morning. I don't know if we'll get through the other four of us now, but there's always tomorrow. We'll see how we get on. Agreed?"

Agreed.

"Okay, who wants to start?"

No one immediately. Given a few seconds more of everyone studying the floor and the ceiling to avoid catching anybody else's eye, I think I might have volunteered, but in the end it was Jenny who spoke first.

"I don't mind beginning," she said evenly.

Relaxation and deep gratitude all round, naturally.

"Go ahead, Jenny," I said, "the floor is yours. What do you fear most?"

Angela threw me an odd glance and a nod after I had said these words. I was in the middle of wondering how much more of this weekend was likely to involve investigations into why women chose to look at me in strange ways, when realization hit me. She was reacting positively to the fact that, for once, I had taken charge.

Jenny smiled round at us all before starting.

"Right. First of all, nothing to do with fears, but earlier on some of you may have noticed my feeble attempt to communicate the fact that I used to be head over heels in love with David when we were in the youth group together, and –"

"Good Lord, so was I!"

Mike's limp-wristed gesture and caricatured effeminate voice made me think of Peter's first "hard thing." What a nightmare.

"And – yes, thank you, Michael – I told him all about it while we were walking on the hills this morning. I confessed I'd been interested to see if those old feelings had completely disappeared – they had, by the way – but I promise you all, I certainly had no intention of mentioning it, because of … because of Jessica. I … well, I sort of got myself into a position where I had to talk about it, didn't I, David?"

A twinge in my most recent guilt wound.

"My fault, Jenny. I chickened out and turned it all on you. Sorry."

"Oh, no, that's fine, honestly. No, I just wanted to come clean, you know."

She cleared her throat a little nervously.

"The thing I'm most afraid of is loneliness."

Me too. Me too. I had a sudden image of walking through my own front door tomorrow and felt sick.

"Very simple. If I think about it too much I get quite frightened by the idea of ending up on my own. Despite what I said when I was telling Mike off earlier, it's not just the physical relationship. It would be nice if that was part of it. What I'd like is someone who's specially mine." She lifted an eyebrow in my direction. "Someone to share the washing-up."

She conducted the silence that followed with her hands.

"I'm afraid that's it, folks. When you get home, if you say prayers, say one for me. Pray that I won't always be alone, but pray even harder that I'll go on following Jesus faithfully if he tells me that he's going to be the only man in my life. Thank you all very much. And – I've so enjoyed being here. I really have. Thank you, Angela. You're such a special person."

Nobody said anything for a while, then Angela spoke.

"Thanks, Jenny. I think we've got a few experts on loneliness sitting round this fire tonight. I'm one. We'll pray about that in the service tomorrow morning, shall we?"

Nods and murmurs of agreement.

"Good. Who's next?"

"Er, does anyone mind if I go next?"

Graham glanced from face to face, a bit-part actor nervously taking the lead for once.

"Go ahead," said Angela.

"Okay." Graham pressed his lips together and swallowed hard several times. Anchoring himself to his chair with both hands, he said, "I'm ... I'm afraid of nothing!"

I didn't altogether blame Mike for his little snort of laughter on hearing this. Given the swallowing, hand-anchoring build-up to Graham's statement, the consistently timid nature of the man, and the hushed, dramatic style of his revelation, I would have been surprised if he had reacted in any other way. The problem for Graham with this response was obvious. It must have been like finally steeling yourself to take a cherished antique or precious stone or heirloom to be valued, and being peremptorily told that it was worth nothing. Jenny smacked Mike's knee. Mike said, "Ow!" and rubbed his leg, pretending it had hurt.

"Don't worry, Graham," said Jenny, "he thought you meant you're not scared of anything. You didn't mean that, did you?"

Distress was instantly chased away by relief on Graham's features.

"Oh, good heavens, no! I'm sorry, Mike. Of course I can see now why you would have thought that. No wonder you laughed. Sorry. I'll start again ..."

I guessed that for him it was always a relief to return to the safe, familiar ground of having something to apologize for.

" ... no, what I was meaning to say was that I'm terrified – yes, I think terrified is the word – of there being nothing after we die. Just lately I've even had trouble sleeping because of it. I lie awake, you see, just thinking about Julie and the girls and all the little things we do and say and feel, and I think to myself – what if it's all rubbish that gets thrown away in the end? What if none of it really means anything? What if there is no God and no heaven and no being together again after we die? And I think, well, if there isn't,

I'd almost rather die now and stop all the pretending and the ... the silly hoping."

His eyes widened and his voice quavered a little as he went on.

"I can't help it. At night, over and over again, I see my little girls' eyes all big and round when they're curled up in their bunks and I'm telling them about Jesus. You know, they look at me with such ... such trust, and believe all the things I say. They ask me questions and I answer them, and they nod. We sing things together and pray. But the trouble is, I'm not sure that I believe what I say. I tell them Grandma's safe in heaven and they're going to see her again one day. But what if she isn't?" His voice rose to a little crescendo, filled with the panic that must have been lying just below the surface for a very long time. "What if it's all just a cruel, nasty joke, and at the end of all these things that seemed to mean so much there's nothing? There are times when – when I want to go to a lonely place and just sort of scream and howl!" He collected himself with an effort and glanced around apologetically. "I don't, of course."

The first line of that poem passed through my mind. "I took my daughter to the park last night ..."

"There is a heaven," said Peter simply, after a short silence, "and Jesus will be there and so will you and your wife and your little girls and their grandma."

"Oh, yes. Yes!" Graham nodded vigorously, as though Peter had proposed a subtle, telling argument that successfully counteracted his fears. "Yes, of course. Thank you."

If there was one thing I had learned from contact with troubled people over the years, it was that spiritual problems are very often not spiritual problems at all. Losing weight, for instance, could be as effective in restoring a faltering relationship with God as anything that the folks at Grafton Manor were able to dish up. There was something else behind Graham's dread of oblivion.

"Graham, do you mind if I ask you something?"

"No, David, not at all, of course not."

"What's your worst worry about you and your family – your very worst worry?"

Graham blinked, then hunted everywhere with his eyes, searching for an escape route that I suspected he didn't really want to find.

"Angela," he said very quietly at last, "I wonder – do you think I might have a glass of wine, or – or whisky even, after I've said what I'm going to say?"

Angela rocked back on her heels and spread her arms expansively. "Graham, the entire contents of the drinks cupboard is at your disposal if you really want it. I made the rule so I can jolly well dump it."

"Thank you. I, er, I don't usually deal with things in that way, you understand."

"No, of course not."

"Right. Good. By the way, the things we say here this weekend, they are – you know – confidential, aren't they?"

We all nodded emphatic agreement. Or anyway, I thought privately, about as confidential as it's possible to get with human beings. When Graham spoke again it was virtually in a whisper.

"Sometimes I long for my family to die."

It was like one of those key moments in a film or a play when one of the characters says something that moves the proceedings in a radically different direction or on to another plane altogether. I hoped no one would feel bound to say anything too quickly in response to this extraordinary statement. They didn't. Graham studied the floor and spread his fingers on the arms of his chair as he went on.

"Sometimes – sometimes I imagine that I'm sitting at home reading a newspaper or listening to Radio Four, and a telephone call comes. When I answer it they tell me that Julie and the girls have all been killed in this bad traffic accident." He glanced up and, lifting one hand from his chair, moved it in a gesture of denial from side to side. "Not – I don't mean one where they're hurt or injured.

Nothing like that. They've just died instantly and at exactly the same moment – suddenly, you know, without even knowing that anything's happened. No pain, no crying, no being afraid. Just – gone. The police stated that death was instantaneous – that's what they say, isn't it? And I get really upset and everything, and we have the funeral and all the people come to the house for ... the get-together, and then they go, and I'm off work for a while with compassionate leave, and then it all settles down and I go back to work and I don't get married again and everything's all right."

Graham's voice filled with emotion as he continued. He was entreating us to understand, to know what it felt like to be inside him.

"You see, the thing is, if it were to happen round about now, if it stopped here, I wouldn't have done too badly, would I? I mean, I've tried very hard and it's been all right. I really have tried. I've tried beyond what I am. It's all not too bad. Julie still loves me. That can't go on forever. It can't! The girls – my girls think I'm really special and funny and okay. They respect me." He shook his head rapidly from side to side. "But they're only little. One day they won't. I know they won't. How on earth could they? I've managed to hold it together up to now. If it ended today or tomorrow or next week I could be at peace for the rest of my life without ever feeling guilty, because it would just be a thing that happened. I could go to work during the day and sit quietly at home in the evening and – and feel sad and listen to the radio." He raised his eyes and looked straight at me. "Do you think I sound like ... like an awful monster, David?"

I couldn't help smiling. "No, Graham, I don't. I'll tell you what you sound like. You sound to me like a very good, very loving man with a very lucky family. You sound like someone who finds it extremely difficult to believe in himself as a husband or as a father. You sound like a man who just can't believe that he's done so well at the things he always thought he'd fail at. You sound like someone who's got his faith wrapped round his fears and needs to do a bit of disentangling.

And as a matter of interest, I happen to know for a fact that you're very far from being alone in thinking the way you do."

"Graham, all that stuff about road accidents," put in Jenny, "if you don't mind me saying so, I think that's just a fantasy, a sort of escape valve to stop you going off pop when you start thinking about the next thirty years instead of keeping your eyes on tonight and tomorrow morning. Fantasies aren't usually about what you really want."

She glanced at me, then back at him.

"Besides, if someone really did give you a choice between your wife and your beloved little girls being there when you get home tomorrow, or discovering that something bad had happened to them while you were away, which would you choose? I mean – look – suppose I really did have the power to make it happen. You choose. You can go home and find they're all dead and gone, killed in that accident you were talking about, or you can have them running up and throwing their arms round you because you're back. Think about it now. Think about their faces. Choose. Which do you want?"

There was no need for him to answer. His face said it all. There was a new light in his eyes. It happens very rarely, but just occasionally the opportunity to confess has an almost instantaneous effect. If it had been a halfway reasonable thing to do, I think Graham might have shot straight out of the door, jumped into his car, and driven through the night to get to the people he loved. Good for him.

"Such a – a relief!" he said. "So silly …"

I braced myself. This time I knew what that glance from Jenny had meant. I drummed a troubled little rhythm on my knees with the flat of my hands before beginning.

"Right, my turn. Earlier in the evening, while we were in the dining room, there were two bits of conversation that never actually led anywhere. One was when Angela asked me if I was willing to talk about Jessica if she talked about Alan, and the other was when Jenny started to say I'd at least begun to do exactly that up on the hills this morning – as well as the, er, stuff about her and me. I was just thinking, Graham, that losing someone you love as much as you love your family and I love my wife would be horrible – is horrible, when it really does happen. It's just plain horrible. There's nothing else to say. There's no way round it, you have to go right through the middle of it. And believe me when I say that you don't end up sitting quietly at home feeling a little bit sad but not too bad really. Fantasies dry up and disappear like ... like that tissue Angela threw on the fire just now. The reality is you fall to pieces inside every day when you wake up and find that it wasn't a nightmare after all.

"Despite all the stuff I do in public I'm not actually that good at talking about how I feel to people I don't know very well, and I came here on Friday pretty determined I wasn't going to talk about my wife whatever happened, but I've changed my mind for all sorts of reasons. And anyway, I'll have to if I'm going to be as honest as Graham has been about what scares me most.

"So, okay, I suppose there are two things I fear most. I'm afraid of living without Jessica, and I'm afraid of living with God without Jessica."

I was aware that Angela had moved so that she was kneeling on the carpet beside my chair, looking up at me as I spoke, letting her arm rest against mine. Surrendering, I laid my face against the wing of my armchair and, for the first time in over eight months, let the words come. If it had been a film, and if there had been music, I think I would have cried like a baby.

"I loved Jessica. I loved Jessica so much. I loved her voice and her walk and her laugh and nearly all the things she did. I loved being at home and in cars and supermarkets and trains and planes and bus shelters and anywhere else with her. I loved her serious sense of duty. And I loved the way she got so excited about enjoying things when she was convinced the time for enjoying things had come and was absolutely right. And I loved – I so loved her being in our house when I came back from being away, seeing her eyes sparkle just be-

cause I had come through the door, and wanting to know all about
how it had gone and what the people were like and what made me
laugh and what I'd had to eat ...

"I loved the fact that we belonged together and we were going
to grow old together. I loved knowing that arguments were never
the end. I loved the way we teased each other about fancying other
people. I loved us praying together and loving God together and saying sorry and talking about what Jesus might have really been like
together, and I really, really loved her face when she was asleep, especially late at night when she'd tried to wait up for me and dropped
off in her armchair, and she'd jump up half awake and try to be all
bright and welcoming when I came in and woke her up, even though
she looked half-crazed and couldn't quite work out where she was
or what was going on. I look into the future, and with no Jessica beside me, my house and my life look so – empty and silent. It's been
frightening me very much."

The fire had burned low and needed to have more wood put on,
but nobody moved. I took a deep breath.

"When she died – she died of a sort of complication from chicken
pox, you know – wouldn't believe it, would you? Septicemia. Chicken
pox. Kid's thing. Sounds so stupid and trivial. When she died I went
home and I sat in the kitchen, and I said to myself – right, you've
been going around for years telling everyone what they ought to
think about God. You've met loads of men and women who've lost
people they love, and you – you've said things to them. Yes, well, go
on! Say them to yourself. See if they help. The expert coach forced
to actually run the bloody marathon. And I went and got a dinner
plate out of the cupboard and deliberately broke it. Against the wall.
I hated myself and I hated God. I hated myself for having a load of
preset answers to all the questions that were flooding through my
brain, all the same old questions that God gets asked by everyone.
Why did she die? What possible good reason could there be for taking her away from me? Why did you give me a job that's so hard to

do on my own if you knew this was going to happen? Why didn't you heal her? Why don't you love me any more? Why don't you exist?

"I found myself hating God for being perfect – someone you can't blame for anything, like a massive face of rock you know you'll never be able to climb because there's nowhere to put your hands or feet. I wanted him to come and be there, sitting at the table with me, visible and caring and real – someone I could touch."

"He was there," said Peter, simply, "hanging on a tree for you, so that you could see Jessica again. He ... he hung on a tree for me this afternoon."

Dear Peter. I was amazed at how my view of him had changed so much in the course of twenty-four hours. Despite everything I couldn't help smiling at his reference to our birch-swinging exploits. It must have been rather puzzling for the others though.

"You're absolutely right. He was there. But I was badly wounded. God may be omnipotent – is omnipotent – but even he wasn't able to actually be Jessica on that day. He didn't try. He took her and then he stood back and waited for me to stop thrashing about and come back to him. I'm glad. I wouldn't want that kind of magic. Grief is real."

I stopped, thinking what a relief it was to begin to discover what I really thought.

"I am frightened about work. I was going to stop. It's going to take me awhile to get back to the sort of thing I've been doing. One thing I don't want is to end up trailing myself around like a sort of bereavement sideshow. I'm all too aware of the way Christian speakers recycle personal tragedy then offer it up as ministry – done it myself. Not any more. If I'm going to carry on I want to preach Christ crucified, not me having a tough time."

"Which plate did you break, David?"

This was greeted with perplexity by the others, and the response took me a moment to think through.

"You're absolutely right," I admitted, "I sorted through the cupboard to find an odd one she wouldn't mind me smashing. Thanks, Jenny."

The answer to Jenny's brilliantly insightful question was a vital aspect of my weekend away. But that was enough from me. Now I wanted to make it easy for Angela. I knew that super-competent characters like her were sometimes not good at the kind of show-and-tell that was going on here. When I touched her hair lightly with my hand she looked up and nodded.

"I'll, er ... I'll put more wood on, shall I?" offered Mike, who had been listening with unusual attentiveness as I spoke.

"Oh, yes. Please, Mike," said Angela. For once there was no smile, and her voice was abnormally quiet and controlled.

Soon the shadows on the old kitchen walls, walls that must have witnessed every possible human emotion in the course of their long history, were dancing in time to the flames that sprang to life almost instantly from the seasoned logs tossed on by Mike.

"I haven't forgotten your whisky, Graham." Without taking her frowning gaze from the fire, Angela lifted an arm and flapped the back of her hand against his leg. "Let me just say my piece and then we'll all have one. You don't mind, do you?"

"Of course, yes, of course – that is – of course not." Graham hastened to reassure her. I was pleased and amazed to see how quickly he had slipped back into his earlier mood of contented relaxation.

We waited.

"Well, basically the bastard dragged my guts out," said Angela at last, still speaking in that low, mechanical voice, "when he drove out of here with that – that girl. I was still all attached to him – important parts of me. He dragged away a chunk of me that I really needed. Well, I mean, that's not fair, is it? Because I need it if I'm going to go on living. It was my stupid fault, of course. I gave it to him. I joined myself to him. I don't know how to get it back."

Her breathing started to escalate as she allowed the anger to rise in her.

"He's a horrible, treacherous, nasty little bastard! I'd like to take one of those logs and smash him as hard as I could with it! I want him to absolutely rot! I want – "

As she turned and looked up at me, her mouth turned down at the corners and her whole face crumpled like a little girl who is too tired to be cross any more and can only manage to cry. The anger in her voice became anguished, tearful puzzlement.

"I thought we were so happy. I loved him. He loved me. I thought it was forever. He went off and left me. I'm never ever going to forgive him – not ever!"

"Yes, you are," said Peter, "because you want to be obedient and you're a very, very beautiful person."

Extraordinary! On hearing this, Angela swung her tear-stained face round in Peter's direction, stared at him in blank incredulity for a moment, then burst into such an explosion of laughter that most of the force went down her nose and Jenny had to leap across and rescue her with an ocean of tissues.

"Oh, Peter!" gasped Angela, when she had scrubbed her face clean and recovered a little, "you are so wonderful, you really are. Not many people would be able to look at a venomous, swearing, unforgiving cow covered in tears and snot and see a very, very beautiful person."

She collapsed into giggles again, as did the rest of us, as much through relief as anything else, I suspected. Peter seemed a trifle bewildered, but he laughed as well, and there was little doubt that he enjoyed his rare excursion into the world of being thought wonderful.

Angela announced that for now she had no more to say about Alan, wisely in my view. She would only have repeated herself.

After that the drinks came out. Graham finally got his whisky, Angela, Jenny, Mike, and I took enormous pleasure in consuming two bottles of quite exceptional white Burgundy that Alan had lovingly put aside for a really important occasion, and Peter was more than happy to be presented with his customary chemical cocktail. From then until bedtime there was a lot of laughter, a lot of relief.

Toast done over the open fire on the end of long forks. Jenny sang to us in Welsh. Mike fell asleep in the corner of the sofa. Graham rang his wife.

Saturday night. We had traveled. We had explored. We hadn't solved much, but we were looking more like human beings, and we had survived.

I was quite unprepared for the wave of unhappiness that swept over me when I finally got up to my bedroom on that Saturday night. My general sense of depression on the previous night had been predictable, but I had hoped against hope that the extraordinary events of the day that had just passed might form a hinge on which my life could at least begin to turn. Whether this was ultimately to be the case or not, as I turned back my covers and climbed into bed, all I could feel was misery and guilt. I had gone walkabout, away from that inner place where, for the last eight months, I had lived with images and memories of Jessica, and made damn sure that the door was rigorously barred against people, things, events, ideas that had no place with us. I felt treacherous. Wretched. I had betrayed our little world, our tiny capsule. Better, surely, if I had ridden my bike straight into the path of the traffic on that day up at Grafton all those months ago.

How could light have turned so quickly to darkness?

After reaching across to switch off my bedside lamp, I let my head fall back on the pillows and stretched an open hand out into the darkness of the room. It was something I had been doing ever since I was a small child, long before I became a Christian. The idea was that, one day, God would take my hand in his, and all would be well forever. He never had taken my hand yet, but I still lived in hope. It was a sort of prayer, I suppose. Tonight, though, I didn't want it to be God who clasped my hand in the darkness. I wanted it to be Jessica. I wanted it to be Jessica!

I dream that I am at the top of the stairs, looking down.

For one glorious beat of my heart I am filled with relief and joy and wonder. For there, standing on the little landing at the bend of the stairs and smiling up at me, is Jessica! It is my Jessica! She is not dead after all. She is alive and smiling. She extends her arms lovingly and begins to climb the stairs toward me. I raise my own arms in welcome, but even as she starts to ascend, troubling thoughts begin to form, unbidden, in my mind.

How could this be my Jessica? Jessica is not alive. Jessica is long dead. Whatever this is coming up the stairs toward me, it is not my wife. This is not real. Oh, but if only I could reach out to touch her, make her real!

It is as if the thing that is making itself look like Jessica has read my thoughts. Just as Jessica is about to reach me, the face that I knew so well and loved so dearly seems to dissolve and melt away to nothing. Jessica is truly gone.

I closed my eyes on my worst nightmare and speak out into the blackness.

"Jesus – Jesus – Jesus – Jesus – Jesus!"

Over and over again I cry out the name of the one who has conquered death and evil. I try to fill my whole being with nothing but his name and his victory and his love. And he hears me. He answers my call on him. His name and his presence work on darkness as liniment works on pain. There is a deep, slow easing of tension and sorrow, until I wake, panting and exhausted, in my room.

I heard you call out, David. Are you okay?"

Such a relief. Oh, such a relief. It was Angela sitting on my bed. I pulled my arms out from under the covers and plonked them down on top of the duvet. Angela was here to comfort me. To make sure I was all right, just as my mother had been there on one isolated, memorable occasion, when, as a nervous small boy, I had cried out at night on waking from a nightmare.

Only I couldn't remember my mother ever looking anything like

Angela. In the subdued light from my little bedside lamp, and in my weakened, vulnerable state, she looked so wonderful that it made me feel quite weepy. She was dressed in a purple silk dressing gown with some kind of Chinese design, very loosely tied at the waist, worn over a long, old-fashioned, cream-colored nightdress made out of very thin material, the kind that is at least as alluring as nakedness on the right woman. With her streaked blonde hair in disarray and not a trace of makeup on her face, energy and kindness and confidence seemed to glow inside and through her like a living flame. Still trembling like a frightened bird from the fear of my nightmare, everything in me wanted to reach out and bury myself and my fears and my loss in the warmth of her face and her body. I had almost forgotten what it meant to really want someone, not only for sex, but for the sensation of being deeply bound up in all that the other person is, weak and strong, adult and child, inside and outside.

I blinked in confusion, licked my dry lips, and decided to lie still.

"I had ... I had an awful nightmare, Angela. Dreadful. Did I really make a loud enough noise for you to hear? I can't believe I did that."

Angela smoothed a loose wisp of hair away from the corner of her mouth and smiled. "Well, it was something between a scream and a groan. A scroan or a gream, perhaps. I thought one of my ghosts must have got you."

"Hm! No, just a dream, but ... well, you know ... one of those nasty, nasty ones."

I turned my head toward the bedside table. "Did you turn my light on, by the way?"

"Yes, when I came in. Why?"

"Oh, nothing ...." I screwed my eyes up and gave my head a little shake, trying to separate strands of nightmare and reality."

Angela stopped smiling and moved closer to me. Lifting my closed right hand from the bed, she held it inside the silk dressing gown against her breasts. With her other hand she stroked my forehead softly. I really did wonder if I might be about to faint. Everything – the room, the bed, Angela and I – seemed to tilt and buzz with repressed energy.

"That really was some nightmare, wasn't it, David?"

"Yes … yes, it was." I could feel my mouth continuing to move but no more words came.

"I'll stay if you want."

"You'll stay."

Her eyes filled with tears.

"Let's be together, David. We've both lost so much. And I need to be close to someone. Just for a little while. I don't … I don't do this, you know."

I knew that if I were to open the hand that Angela was holding so very, very lightly against the softness of her body, I would be lost. My lips felt drier than ever. Nevertheless, the madman must speak.

"Angela – oh, Angela! I'm afraid there's only a tiny part of me that's strong enough to say this, and if you stay much longer I won't be able to, but – look, it would make a mockery of everything. It would mean – I don't know – it would mean Jenny was talking nonsense earlier. It would mean you and I had given in. It would mean Peter's giving half his life away for nothing. I believe it all, Angela. I really do. And I know you do as well. I know I'm going to want you to come back the instant you go out of that door, but – please – please, for both our sakes, please won't you just go."

Angela smiles a watery smile and nods. Lifting my hand in both of hers she kisses it once before releasing it. She stands, secures her dressing gown by its red and blue cord, and leaves, closing the door behind her as she goes.

After she has gone the anger and the relief roll and wrestle violently around the floor and the walls and the ceiling of this room that I have not coolly but quite deliberately made into a dungeon.

I am angry. I am angry because I have refused an opportunity to feel the warm body and mind of a beautiful person against my body and mind when it is what I need and yearn for. I weep. I have given away the chance to hold and be held, awake and asleep. I have surrendered touch and tongues and caresses and kisses and murmurs and sighs and ripples of laughter. Those smiling eyes and that soft mouth might have been mine for the space of a night. My heart, my skin, my loneliness cry out for the solace that I have rejected. Oh, Jesus!

I am relieved. I am relieved because I know that the morning will follow the night, and morning will bring a white light flooding into dark places. It will reveal those things that we knew full well were there but chose to ignore because they threatened to thwart us. I am relieved. I am relieved because I love him. Yes, beneath the anger and the grief and the disappointment and the fear and the foreboding I love him as I have loved him for so many years. He is my Lord. I am his servant – and his friend if I obey him. I so long to be angry with him like a child for allowing all those nights and this night to come upon me, but I know he would do more – has done immeasurably more for me than I shall ever do for him. Oh, Jesus!

Let me hear Jessica's voice and hold her hand once more, I pray. But let your will be done. And forgive this, my silly prayer.

Anger and relief. The night rages on. But it is hardly Gethsemane.

CHAPTER SIX
Sunday

White light, relief, and rain. In the morning the anger had gone, but these three remained. Outside my window a steady drizzle had set in, creating the sort of atmosphere that is cosily dramatic and delicious, or dismally dull and dreary, depending on your relationship with weather. Today, I loved it. After getting dressed I settled down by the window to plan my talk for the service.

Coming down for breakfast later, I met Angela at the bottom of the stairs, looking as miraculously full of energy and inner light as ever. She was wearing light-blue jeans, a big, soft, off-white man's jumper and a dark-blue bandanna tied around her head. She was made for hugging. I hugged her. She held on to me for a moment, drawing her head back so that she could look me in the eye.

"By the way, I was only kidding last night, you know. I didn't really want to stay."

I nodded seriously. "Oh, I know. So was I. I didn't really want you to stay either."

She put her face next to mine again and whispered, "Thank you, David."

Graham said the obvious but perennially true thing at breakfast.

"It seems a shame, doesn't it? Just as we're really getting to know each other and starting to relax, it's time to go home."

A comfortable position to be in if home is a place you love. It could be a good feeling to be cushioned between the two soft places of what is to be and what has just been. I had known that feeling in the past. I was glad for him. It wasn't quite like that for me nor, I strongly suspected, for Jenny and Peter. I wasn't sure about Mike. A lonely man. Interestingly, I felt that, of all the others, Mike was the one I knew less about now than I had at the beginning of the weekend. It was probably something to do with his readiness to change shape. Social chameleons with a tendency toward flippancy are an elusive breed. And they weary people. Perhaps I would have a chance to chat with him just before leaving, after the communion.

By ten o'clock all our bags had been piled in the hall ready for "the off," as Jessica so hated it being called, and we were gathered around the dining room table in exactly the positions that we had occupied on Saturday night, except that Angela made me swap places with her so that I could sit at the end, facing Mike. A plate with part of a French bread lying on it and an earthenware goblet filled with wine waited in the center of the table.

Today the fire was dead, and the rain continued unabated, battering away at the long grass outside the old leaded windows, but there was definitely a hint of a glow around us on that Sunday morning.

Jenny and Graham had spent part of Saturday afternoon putting together the service that was to provide the context in which we broke bread together. It was a very simple one, mostly drawn from the prayer book, but one strange thing happened during a lingering silence after the prayer of confession. An infectious ripple of laughter ran around the table, and then was gone as if it had never happened. Strange. Interesting. Good.

Suddenly it was time for the address that Angela had asked me to deliver, my first talk to any group of people since before Jessica's death. Right up to the moment of waking that morning, I had entertained the gravest doubts about my ability to go through with this. Now I was nervous but calm. I looked round at the faces of my five companions and began.

R ight, well, it's generous and brave of you to ask me to be the one to speak this morning. I haven't done anything like this since February, so I'm probably a bit rusty.

"Er, I was just thinking that some prayers can't be answered. In the early hours of this morning, for instance, I told God how much I would love to be with Jessica and hold her hand one last time. That's not going to happen, of course, but fortunately it's not my only prayer. My other prayer, and it's only really come to life this weekend, is that I should survive and be of some use. The things I thought I'd say to you and myself this morning are the beginnings of an answer to that prayer, and for as long as I can remember I've been under strict orders from – well, from lots of people when I think about it, my father when I was a child, my wife when I became a man, and God since I was sixteen years old, to share the things that I've been given. So that's what I'm going to do. I hope it's all right. And, you'll be pleased to hear, I've got a text! That's a relief, isn't it?"

Cheers and applause from around the table.

"I don't know if your experience has been the same as mine – but have you noticed how some bits of the Bible stay more or less invisible for years? And then, for no apparent reason, it's as though some unseen hand reaches down and places that special little group of words in front of your eyes in such a clear, graphic way that you simply have to take notice of them. A sort of heavenly Braille, in a way, I suppose, especially when you think that spiritual blindness can only ever be removed by the grace of God. Well, that's what happened to me early this morning when I was sitting in my bedroom trying to think what on earth I was going to say to you lot.

"I was thumbing through the New Testament when I came across the bit in chapter seven of Matthew's gospel where Jesus says that we mustn't cast our pearls before swine. I suddenly really, really wanted to understand what he meant when he said that. It felt terribly important. In fact, and you're going to think this is incredibly stupid, I got so wrapped up in the whole issue that, in the end, I told myself off. Forget all that, I said. Put the pearls and swine thing on one side until you've come up with something to speak about at the communion. Well then, thank God, sanity set in, and I took the hint, if that's what it was. So, when I'd finally given myself permission to think about it, these were the questions that went rolling round my head.

"What pearls?

"What swine?

"What's the problem with feeding the poor old latter with the useless old former?

"So, as I thought about all this a kind of understanding began to form in my mind. Don't get me wrong, I'm not for one minute pretending I've got the one and only true answer to those questions. My interpretation of what Jesus said is bound to be more or less subjective, especially at the present time, I suppose. But what I did find is that this verse might have something very important to say about the things that have happened to me this weekend, and I'm hoping you'll sort through my rubbish and find something helpful for you as well. At the very least I hope you'll find something to send your thinking off into all sorts of other areas, ones that are just as useful as mine, or more so.

"Right – enough of the defensive stuff. First of all, I thought I'd better make sure I knew what pearls actually were. So I nipped downstairs and looked them up in the 'P' section of that set of massive brown encyclopaedias in Angela's library that probably haven't been read since they were bought and are going to break the shelf they're sitting on any decade now, Angela.

"Apparently pearls are formed by oysters as a reaction or defense against a foreign body or irritant, usually a piece of sand or grit, getting into the soft tissues. Bluish-gray layers form round the unwanted invader, and the final product of all these repeated accretions is a hard, translucent gem that's always been regarded, by us human beings at least, as a thing of great beauty and high monetary value. End of pearl lecture.

"Interesting, though, because I think something very similar has happened in my own life – and yours. There've been troubles and weaknesses and negative influences that haven't just threatened but come very close to moving in and ruining parts of my life. I guess most of these – irritants or whatever you like to call them, go back to childhood, but as you know, their effect is timeless. Not very long ago, for instance, I was walking along one of the big London shopping streets, and I just caught a glimpse of a particular pattern of material in a shop window. Believe it or not, it was enough to trigger a few seconds of real misery – no, let's face it – anguish and rage, about something my mother did or said thirty-odd years ago, when I was four or five years old. Sometimes it could be the tone in a person's voice or just a pattern of clouds in the sky. It only lasts for seconds, but the effect is as dramatic and momentarily blinding as the flash going off on a camera. I know how absurd all that must sound to those who've never been through it, but for some people it's simply a fact of life.

"For me, of course, the most recent and easily the most negative influence has been the death of my wife. As you all know, losing Jessica introduced me to experiences that were ... well, they were completely new. In the past I'd heard people talk about losing the will to live, but it wasn't until the moment I walked through the front door of our – my house after leaving the hospital on the day she died, that I came anywhere near understanding what they were on about. Facing the pain every single day is such a terrible thing, and the nights have brought some terrible dreams.

"I confess I came to join you for this weekend with a heart full of confusion and anger and stubbornness. I was coldly determined nothing would break into or out of the shell that was preventing me from handing my wife over to God, and God from giving me courage and hope for the future. Well, nothing's changed very much. I'm really dreading getting home this evening. It's the first time I've been away and come back since Jessica died. And I'm dreading going up to bed tonight because half the room will be empty and – oh, dear! – I'll have to decide whether to turn her bedside light on or not. It'll go on being tough, I know it will, but the crucial difference is this. I think – I think I've given up. I mean, I think I've given up the idea that I might sort it out for myself. I've tried to do it on my own, but I can't do it. There's a grand tradition of little kids trying to do grown-up things before they're ready, and then having to go back to their dads and say, 'I'm sorry, I can't do it. Will you do it for me?' I think that's what I've done, and I'm glad.

"And of course I'm not alone. We all have our difficult dark invaders, don't we? Looking round now I think of what we've shared this weekend, and how brave we're all going to need to be. I know that we've only touched the surface of each other's lives, but you have inspired me, you really have. Thank you. Thank you for all sorts of things, not least for reminding me how important physical things can be, like wrestling with doors in the middle of storms and long walks on hills and leaping suicidally off the tops of trees.

"I'm sure we shouldn't take any pride or satisfaction in these irritants that enter our lives, but, look, I do think we should greatly value the way in which God's able to form a pearl of protection around each of them. He hasn't got rid of most of them because he's good enough to allow us to go on being the person we are. We wear God's pearls as symbols of our vulnerability and perhaps as pictures of the way God can make something beautiful out of weakness.

"Speaking for myself, in practical terms this has meant I've been willing to own my problems and weaknesses in any public speaking I've done. Knowing that vulnerability isn't a sin – and Jesus himself is the clearest example of that – can be very helpful to people who've been intimidated by 'perfect' Christians.

"I'm proud of my pearls, and so should you be proud of yours.

"So, who are the swine?

"Well, it's interesting. In this context they've tended to be Christians who suffer from what seems an overwhelming compulsion to put me right. They get very agitated when I appear too casually open about deficiencies in my Christian life or the way my personality and experience are affected by things from the distant past. I know they think they're being helpful when they send me books or tapes or leaflets that might address my problems, but they've actually got it wrong. You see, they want to heal my uncertain childhood and my skepticism toward most human organizations, and my habit of hanging about on the edge of things, waiting to see if the truth will end up inside or outside the circles that nervous Christians like us seem obliged to form all the time. I don't want them healed, thanks very much, any more than a red-haired person wants the color of his hair healed or a left-handed person wants his left-handedness cured or a person who likes singing in the bath wants that habit drawn out of them by the roots, like some sort of wart.

"I truly think one of the most wonderful things God offers us is his permission to follow Jesus without becoming somebody else. Paul the apostle, for instance, didn't change from being exactly the man he'd been before his Damascus Road experience, but a brand-new, God-given perspective redirected all his energies and talents and tendencies toward a completely different goal.

"These helpful swine want to get rid of anything that makes you or me different from the kind of person that actually only exists in the context of those strange acts of corporate dishonesty that some Christian congregations specialize in.

"So why do they do it?

"Difficult to be sure, but I think this obsession with spiritual blandness comes from a mixture of fear and unbelief. I read somewhere that insecure church leaders are like children left in charge of a house. They get so worried about the size of the job that they make up a set of horrendously impossible rules for each other in order to cope. It's just an attempt to control a situation that feels frighteningly complex. People who are frantic to get others fixed are often plagued with worry and doubt in exactly the same way. The bad news for them is that they'd have found Jesus terribly worrying two thousand years ago. The even worse news for them is that he hasn't changed at all.

"Graham, Jenny, Angela, Mike, Peter, we can only follow Jesus as we are, just like the old disciples had to. Me with the hole left in my life by Jessica's death, Graham with insecurities about being a husband and father, insecurities that leak into his faith, Jenny with her fear of loneliness, Angela with the need to forgive and get rid of all the bitterness inside her, Mike with his feeling that God has never shown him how much he loves him, and Peter ..."

I looked a question at Peter. Paler than ever, he nodded resolutely.

"And Peter with the fact that he's gay – "

A murmured ripple of response.

"Peter with the fact that he's gay and has made a decision to remain celibate for the rest of his life. All sorts of people have all sorts of views on that, but they're not important. This is what he's decided and I respect him for it. Yesterday Peter actually did the thing he's been most frightened of all his life. He very bravely told someone what I've just told you. For the first time ever, wasn't it, Peter?"

"Mm."

"Like I said, we follow Jesus with all that baggage on our backs, and we hope and pray that God will do something to ease our burdens. But we don't give up just because we're not as good at forgiving ourselves as God is at forgiving us. In any case, the problems are only a part of us. There are all the strengths and the talents and the beautiful things about each of us, and they have to go in the rucksack as well.

"Pearls are valuable things. They're beautiful, and they're what you get when God transfigures things that could have turned very ugly. Whatever we do, we mustn't let anyone take them away from us. And now, I'm getting sick of the sound of my own voice, so I'll say – amen."

The prayers that we said for each other before passing round the bread and wine that morning were nourishing, perhaps as nourishing as the communion itself. There was no pressure on anyone to pray aloud, but everybody except Mike said something. Peter prayed for Andrew.

Most moving of all for me was Jenny's prayer for Peter. She got up and moved down the table so that she could stand behind his chair and wrap her arms round his neck like a human scarf. Laying her face on his shoulder, she thanked God for him and prayed that he would find lots and lots of love in his life and be exactly the person he was supposed to be. Then she stood up, kissed him on the very top of his head, and returned to her seat. For at least a minute or two after that there were traces of color in Peter's bloodless cheeks. The peace in his eyes lasted for much longer.

As we passed the bread and the wine to each other, they were, to us, the body and blood of Christ. We took them and ate and drank them in the knowledge that they were given for us, we remembered that Christ died for us, and we fed on him in our hearts by faith with thanksgiving.

B ecause of the rain, good-byes happened in the hall. They happened quite quickly and were conducted with passion and strain. We hardly knew each other. It had been very intense. Now we were parting. Addresses and numbers were busily exchanged. Half-formed arrangements were left to be finalized at some later date. Open invitations were extended.

Well, perhaps some of us would meet again. I hoped so, but I had been part of too many weekends away to be very sure of that.

I had decided to be the last to go. Graham and Jenny were the first. He had picked her up on his way over on Friday and would now take her home. I shook hands with Graham, encouraged him, and wished him well. He was bright-eyed and positively throbbing with excitement about the prospect of going home to his beloved family. How much would he tell Julie about what had happened this weekend? Not too much. Just enough.

I didn't think Jenny looked at all excited about the idea of going home. I told her how much I admired her, which I did, and how grateful I was for her part in changes that had begun in me this weekend. I told her how much I liked her red hat and she laughed. She told me she would never forget our walk over the hills. Then she looked as if she might cry and hurried after Graham out into the yard.

For traveling back to Yorkshire, Peter had elected to wear a navy-blue blazer with silver buttons, worn over a dark pink roll-neck sweater made from some thin acrylic material. He looked as if he was off to judge a dog show. Whatever had peeped out during the weekend seemed to have retreated for now. The big bad world was out there, and it was tough. He shook hands with me over-politely, pecked Angela on the cheek, and ducked his tall form out of the door.

Mike, wearing his heavy cord trousers and leather jacket, had hung about by the door, saying good-bye to the others and flicking a glance at Angela every now and then. Sensing that there was something he wanted to say to Angela without anyone else being around, I took up a stance in the porch, gazing out across the wet yard. A few minutes later there was a loud burst of merriment from Angela, followed by the sound of a hand slapping leather two or three times. Moments later, Mike, with a rueful expression on his second-hand features, caught my arm, spun me round, and stuck a hand out.

"See yer, mate!" he said.

I poked a folded piece of paper into his top pocket as I shook his hand.

"If you ever feel like getting in touch, give us a ring." I meant it.

"Right."

"Mike, just before you go – as a matter of interest, after this weekend, everything that's happened, what do you – I don't know how to put it – where do you stand with Christianity?"

He pondered, blowing his cheeks out and knitting his brows.

"It's been a laugh," he said eventually, "it's been good. At the end of the day, though, well, it's crap, right? I mean – Jenny and Peter whipping themselves to death for wanting a spot of the other like everyone else. Why? What's that all about?" He looked thoughtful for a moment. "Oh, I dunno! Anyway – cheers, mate." Pause. "Sorry about Jess. Cheers, Angela!"

Angela came and stood beside me in the doorway, arms folded, watching as Mike climbed into his battered old Peugeot and chugged noisily away out of the yard.

"Mike's in love with me," she said. "Well, he was until two minutes ago. Now he's not."

I chuckled. "Yes, I heard you smacking some sense into him. Poor old Mike. I hope he does give me a ring sometime."

"So do I. Here you are, David." Angela offered me a white envelope.

"What's this?"

"It's from Jessica. It's only a letter."

Only a letter. Only a letter from Jessica. I took it, and without thinking, raised it to my lips.

"You'd better be off."

Turning round into the hall, Angela picked up my bag, hefted it out and across the yard, and slung it on to the backseat of my unlocked car. I hadn't moved. She came back to the doorway, one hand smoothing her glistening wet hair.

"Find a place on the way home, David. Bye. God bless."

I came out of my trance.

"Yes. Angela. Good-bye. Thanks."

Jessica's friend, Angela. She smiled and lifted her face to kiss me gently on the cheek, then she spun me round and gave me a little push with both hands in the direction of my car. As I started it up and pulled away, still in a trance-like state, she was standing in the doorway, arms folded once more, still smiling. She lifted one hand in salute as I turned out of the yard and set off down the drive toward the lane.

I found a pub on the way back. I took my drink to a corner by the window and sat quietly for a while, watching the rain stream off a blocked gutter just outside. Jessica's unopened letter lay on the polished table in front of me. Several times I extended a hand and then snatched it back again immediately. Once I had read this letter it would have been – read. Perhaps it would be better if I never read it. I could keep it on a shelf in our kitchen and just let it be part of my life. I could do that. I picked it up at last, raised it to my lips once more, then lowered it, and forced the envelope open with my finger. Taking out the thin sheets of handwritten paper, I carefully unfolded them and began to read.

My dearest, darling David,

I do hope you've found a really nice place to sit and read my last letter to you. I think if things had happened the other way round I would probably have chosen somewhere out of doors. Yes, thinking about it, I definitely would. And it could rain if it wanted to. I wouldn't mind. I'd love to be in the rain one more time. You and I always loved all sorts of different weather, didn't we? Or rather I always did and you often did and had to pretend sometimes. So, maybe just for my sake you're sitting under a tree on a nice dry waterproof, all dressed up warm and holding that big green golfing umbrella of ours to keep the rain off your hair. You don't like getting your hair wet, do you, darling? It makes you so ratty.

Isn't it nice to be together one last time as you read this? I hope it is. I wish with all my heart that I could be with you properly, David, but it's only just sunk in over the last couple of hours that we shan't be together for very much longer, and so I wanted to find a way to be with you just once more after I've gone. I know you won't be able to see me or touch me, but honestly, I don't reckon I shall be all that far away as you read this. If it's allowed (who knows what's allowed?) I'm going to come as close to you as I can and snuggle up under the umbrella and watch your face as you read and probably wish I'd written a better letter than this. Oh, dear, I'm starting to sound as if I'm in one of those weepy films you always enjoyed so much, aren't I? Do you remember I laughed once about you blubbering, didn't I, and you got very serious indeed and told me I didn't understand.

You said that every time you were made to feel something very intensely it was such a relief because then you believed that you were alive again. Do you remember that? I'm still not sure what you were talking about...

I love you so much.

David, it isn't dying I mind so much. Honestly. I'm surprised. Now it comes to it, I feel ever so peaceful about me. I'm a little bit afraid of how much it might hurt, but I'm pretty sure I actually do believe all the things that we said we believed every Sunday and all the other times. Anyway, right or wrong, by the time you read this I shall know all about it, and – by gosh! – won't you be just hating the thought of that. As far as you're concerned we always did have to discover things together, didn't we, darling? You always get so cross whenever you have to play catch-up with me. Not this time, though. By the time you take this letter out of its envelope, I shall be with Jesus, wondering how we could all have been so dense, and seeing some amazing, beautiful things. But we will be together later on. It's a promise. Not mine.

No, the thing I do mind terribly is leaving you, my precious, precious husband. I just had to stop writing for a minute or two because I couldn't keep the tears from coming when I thought of you raging like a blizzard inside, your face all set and expressionless because, as I know only too well, you won't have a clue about what to do with all the hurt and loneliness that's washing around inside you. Not a bit like a soppy film I'm afraid, is it, my darling?

And then I think of you waking up in the morning and wondering if it was all a nightmare and turning your head very slowly to see if I'm there beside you like I have been so many times since the day we got married. And then rolling your head back and staring at the ceiling, trying to work out new ways to get yourself through another whole twenty-four hours. Hey! I've just thought of one good thing – you can have as many pillows as you like now, and there won't be any more of those midnight tug-o'-war sessions with the duvet, that I could only win by kicking you really hard in the leg.

I wish we could be in bed together once more.

I've thought of another good thing. You'll be able to pay off the house. It'll be ours – I mean, yours – at last!

I hope you won't mind me rambling on like this, but I don't want to leave anything out. There are four other important things I want to say to you, darling.

First, I want to thank you very much for our marriage. Hasn't it been nice? Well, it has been pretty good, hasn't it? I hope you've enjoyed it. We've had lots of fun in lots of different ways. A few problems and a few end-of-the-world rows, but nothing that didn't culminate in the rapture. (That's supposed to be a joke, by the way, in case you didn't get it.) David, be sad about the immediate future if you like, but not about the past. We may not have made our twentieth anniversary, but the years we had were good, rich ones. I'd like you to know that it was a pleasure and a privilege to spend them with you. That may sound a bit silly and formal, but I don't care because I mean it.

Secondly, I wanted to say something about the future. I know that in quite a few of those films that you have such a strangely unaccountable affection for, dying wives make their husbands swear that they'll marry again, within a week or so of being bereaved usually, isn't it? Right now I'm afraid I don't feel like that at all. The worst part of me, the bad Jessica, wants you to love me and think about me and want me and grieve for me and not even notice any other women for the rest of your life until the day you die and join me in heaven and I can start nagging you all over again. But the best Jessica, the good Jessica, doesn't want that. I know you're going to be very unhappy, just as I would have been if you'd died, but you won't be sad forever, sweetheart. One morning you're going to wake up and feel a bit guilty and troubled because the pain isn't quite as bad as it was before, and that'll be the first stage of being somewhere near all right again, and after that – well, I have to grit my teeth and say that, as you'd be absolutely useless at being on your own, I want you to find someone else one day. And I mean that as well. You'll have my blessing and my love, and let me tell you that she will be a very lucky lady indeed. You will tell her what you do to the toothpaste tube at a very early stage in the relationship though, darling, won't you?

The third thing is about this letter and why I'm going to send it to Angela to give to you. I'm not totally sure myself why I want to do that, except that she was a big part of the days when it all started for us, wasn't she? Part of us getting converted, whatever that meant – words are getting sillier and sillier by the hour – and part of you and me coming together a bit later on. You fancied Angela something rotten in the old days, didn't you? You can smile! I do hope you're blushing as well, David Herrick. Mind you, you weren't alone, I can assure you. Most of the boys turned into little tail-wagging puppies every time she looked at them or spoke to them. I didn't mind. She was lovely, and she was my bestest friend coming up through school. Always so confident and strong and sweet-natured with it. Over the last few years our lives only touched through Christmas cards, as you know, but she's never stopped being special to me. Somehow, she seems the obvious person to send this to. I'm going to ask her to give you this letter a few months after I'm gone, at a moment that seems absolutely right to her. I have no idea how she'll organize it, but you and I know that Angela always did have her own interesting way of doing things. I expect I'll speak to her on the phone, but I've told her in my letter not to reply to me in case you find it. I want this to be a surprise and a comfort to you, my darling, hopefully at a time when you really need it. Do give dear Angela a hug and a kiss for me.

Here's my fourth point. Have you got fed up with the rain and gone inside somewhere now? David, please go on telling people about Jesus. Go on telling the truth and helping people to understand that God loves them. We can only be good and obedient when we know we're loved, can't we, and that's the job God's specially given you. To make sure that all the silliness and the messing about doesn't cover up the fact that the best and most important thing in the world is waiting for us if we really want it. Let's face it, I shall be personally proving how important it is at the precise moment when you read this sentence! Be angry, be sad, rave and rage at God about losing me, if you have to, but don't ever stop telling the truth, my darling. I know you've always felt inadequate when you've been silly enough to measure yourself against your message, but that's why people listen to you. I had a dream about you and Jesus last night, that I'm not allowed to tell you about, but I can tell you that it would make you cry and it would make you very happy, a bit like your silly old films. I know where your heart is – so do you.

I'm running out of oomph, my dear friend – husband – lots of things. I'd like to write love love love love love all over a blank page, but it would just look silly. I'm ever so tired. Do something for me. Close your eyes and pretend you're holding my hand for a moment. Did you do that? So did I. God bless, sweetheart. You sleep well tonight.

Jessica

P.S. David, you haven't forgotten to water my plants, have you?

Adrian Plass is one of today's most significant and successful Christian authors and speakers. Among his many popular books are *The Sacred Diary of Adrian Plass Aged 37 ¾*; *The Sacred Diary of Adrian Plass, Christian Speaker Aged 45 ¾*; *The Sacred Diary of Adrian Plass, on Tour*; *The Theatrical Tapes of Leonard Thynn*; *The Horizontal Epistles of Andromeda Veal*; *The Growing-up Pains of Adrian Plass*; *And Jesus Will Be Born*; *The Final Boundary*; *View from a Bouncy Castle*; *The Visit*; *A Year at St. Yorick's*; *Stress Family Robinson*; and *Jesus—Safe, Tender, Extreme*. Known for his ability to evoke both tears and laughter, he has been reaching the hearts of thousands for more than twenty years. He lives in East Sussex, England, with his wife, Bridget.

Jesus – Safe, Tender, Extreme

Adrian Plass

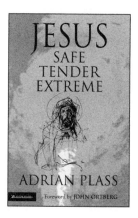

Evocative reflections on three facets in our relationship with Jesus.

People long for reality in their walk with Christ. To know him better, we must understand the different sides of his complex nature. Popular British author Adrian Plass draws on biblical stories and personal experience – as well as his keen understanding of people's needs – as he explores the Safe Jesus, the Tender Jesus, and the Extreme Jesus. God has told us that he holds us in the palm of his hands, where no one and nothing can harm the most important part of us. But from biblical times to the present day, Christians encounter accidents and disasters. What does it really mean to experience the Safe Jesus? Jesus tells his disciples that they must love one another. Yet time and again we try to find achievement and success through our own efforts and individual gifts, only to end in failure. Instead, we need to know the Tender Jesus who becomes visible when we join with each other in the body of Christ. Jesus only did what he saw his father doing. Each of his actions and encounters were fueled, informed, and instructed by the dynamic, creative, unpredictable Spirit of God. Failing to be obedient in this way is what truly constitutes sin. When we are open to the genuine leading of the Spirit, we will experience the Extreme Jesus.

In *Jesus – Safe, Tender, Extreme*, Adrian Plass is "simply a man with a broom, sweeping away the rubbish that prevents others from passing further in and further up, by talking about what Jesus does and doesn't do in my life."

Hardcover, Jacketed: 978-0-310-25784-4

And Jesus Will Be Born

A Collection of Christmas Poems, Stories and Reflections

Adrian Plass

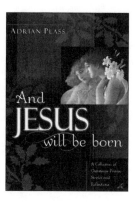

In this gentle and humorous anthology of poems, stories, commentary and reflections, Adrian Plass invites us to celebrate Christmas in its many facets. *And Jesus Will Be Born* is a holiday cornucopia filled with the laughter, tears, family foibles, simple joys and the rich blessings of the season.

There's no predicting what the turn of a page will bring in this Christmas collection by Adrian Plass. It may be a bit of verse to moisten the eyes ...

Then again, there is this — an 'advertisement' from Plass's spoof of a church newsletter:

'How beautiful on the mountains are the feet of those who bring good news? The answer is — not very, if they haven't had those ugly corns treated. Christian chiropodist. Special Yuletide reductions ...'

Setting the poignant, the madcap, the joyous and the tender in artful counterpoint, this is a book to be savored over the entire holiday season. It offers something for everyone in every setting — family readings, personal libraries and even church pulpits.

And Jesus Will Be Born speaks to the full spectrum of our humanity, celebrating the golden Christmas traditions, poking playfully at our seasonal foibles, observing our less-than-noble attitudes with an eye that is at once honest and gracious — and always looking towards the Person around whom all that is truly Christmas revolves.

In the midst of our festivities, Adrian Plass gently reminds us why we need a Savior. And he points us towards the unfathomable possibilities that have been opened to us, and the joy and hope that are ours, because Jesus was born long ago in Bethlehem and is born today in us.

Hardcover, Jacketed: 978-0-00-713051-1

Share Your Thoughts

With the Author: Your comments will be forwarded to the author when you send them to *zauthor@zondervan.com*.

With Zondervan: Submit your review of this book by writing to *zreview@zondervan.com*.

Free Online Resources at
www.zondervan.com

Zondervan AuthorTracker: Be notified whenever your favorite authors publish new books, go on tour, or post an update about what's happening in their lives.

Daily Bible Verses and Devotions: Enrich your life with daily Bible verses or devotions that help you start every morning focused on God.

Free Email Publications: Sign up for newsletters on fiction, Christian living, church ministry, parenting, and more.

Zondervan Bible Search: Find and compare Bible passages in a variety of translations at www.zondervanbiblesearch.com.

Other Benefits: Register yourself to receive online benefits like coupons and special offers, or to participate in research.